VICTOR LOPEZ AT THE ALAMO

VICTOR LOPEZ AT THE ALAMO

Written and Illustrated
by James Rice

PELICAN PUBLISHING COMPANY
Gretna 2001

*The word "Pelican" and the depiction of a pelican are trademarks
of Pelican Publishing Company, Inc., and are registered in the
U.S. Patent and Trademark office.*

Library of Congress Cataloging-in-Publication Data

Rice, James, 1934-
    Victor Lopez at the Alamo / written and illustrated by James
Rice.
        p. c.m.
    Summary: Victor, a fourteen-year-old Mexican boy, is abducted by
Mexican soldiers marching to Texas to put down the uprising
there and experiences the Battle of the Alamo.
    ISBN: 1-56554-866-3 (alk. paper)
    1. Alamo (San Antonio, Tex.)—Siege, 1836—Juvenile fiction. [1.
Alamo (San Antonio, Tex.)—Siege, 1836—Fiction. 2. Texas—
History—To 1846—Fiction.] I. Title.

PZ7.R3634 Vi 2001
[Fic]—dc21
                                                        00-054855

Printed in The United States of America
Published by Pelican Publishing Company, Inc.
1000 Burmaster Street, Gretna, Louisiana 70053

1

It STARTED just this morning.

The soldiers. Endless columns of them. Dusty, tired soldiers.

Victor watched as the slow procession passed his family's modest *caseta*. The troops paid little attention to the boy as they stared straight ahead, placing one weary foot in front of the other.

The late winter chill of the previous night had barely changed to the warmth of mid-morning. The soldiers' once dark blue tunics and white trousers were now gray with dust and spotted with perspiration stains. Many had discarded the heavy tunics and hard, uncomfortable *tapas* for the simple peasant costume of light cotton shirts, trousers, and straw hats. They bore little resemblance to a military organization with their short-barreled muzzleloaders carried loosely in relaxed positions. Each found his most comfortable way to handle the awkward pieces of equipment.

The soldiers most nearly resembling a formal military unit were mounted on horses. Their once bright red and blue uniforms were now shades of gray under heavy layers of dust like their counterparts on foot, but their swords and pistols were of much newer vintage.

Victor had never before seen anything like this in his young life. He, Mama, and El Viejo, his uncle, lived on their little piece of land far from any neighbors. El Viejo had found the small, spring-fed stream and had claimed

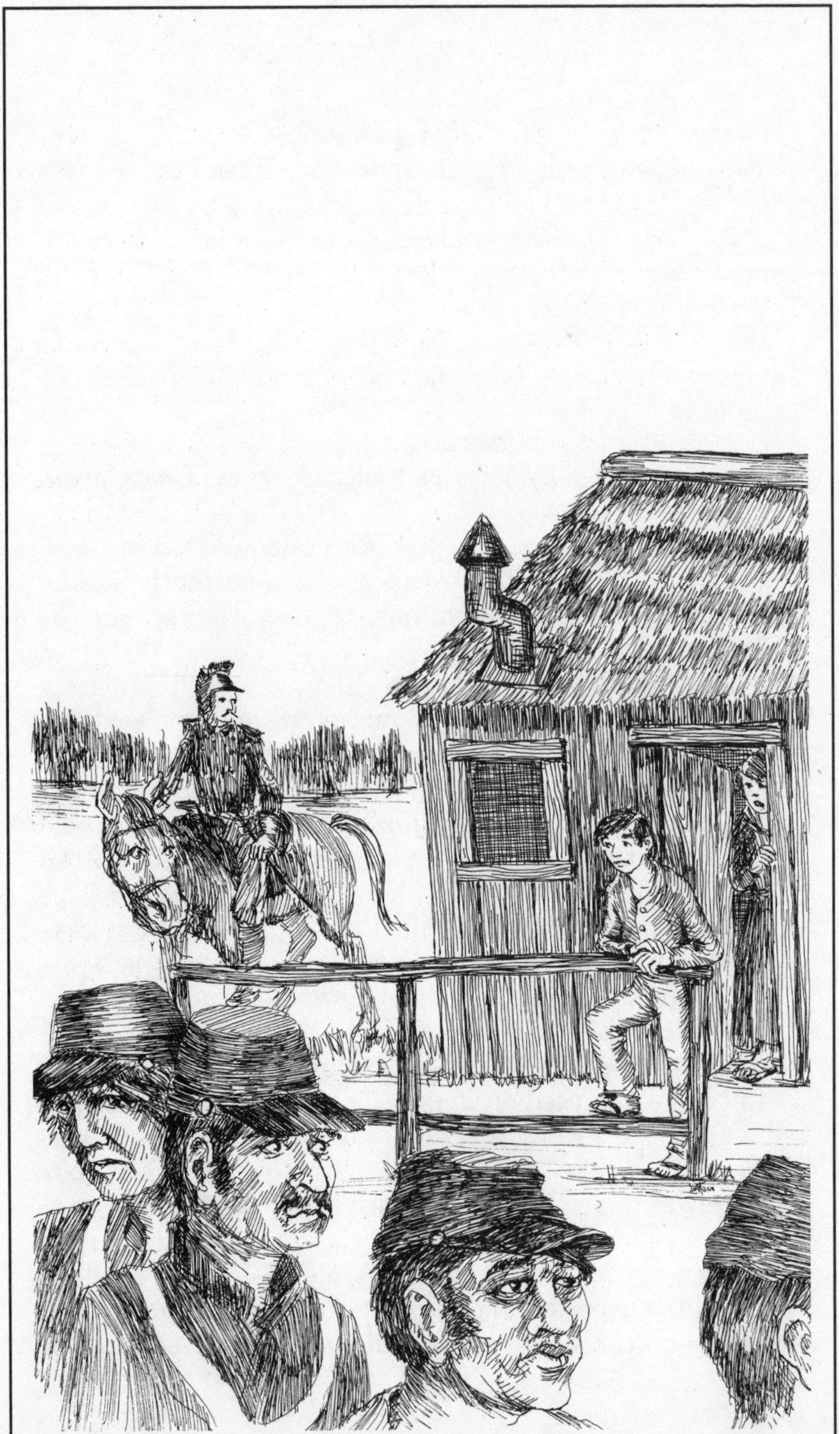

it, along with a small plot of surrounding land, for his own. Although he had no papers saying he owned this property, no one had ever disputed his claim.

By most people's standards he and his family lived in poverty, but Victor didn't know they were poor. They did not want for necessities. Their little garden provided plenty of beans and corn for the tortillas. They had goats, pigs, and chickens for milk, cheese, meat, and eggs. Who could ask for more?

They had very little money, but then where could they spend it? They traded for anything they needed that their little farm did not provide.

"Victor!" his mother called. "Victor!"

"Yes Mama, I'm coming," he answered.

"Victor, pen the chickens early tonight and tie the goats out in the brush behind the pig pen, out of sight of the road. As of last night, two chickens are missing."

"*Qué pasa,* Mama? Are the coyotes prowling again?"

Mama cut her eyes and flashed a humorless smile, "Yes, my son, but these are the two-legged kind who wear uniforms and march the roads." Her smile faded. "I wish we could help them—your father died wearing the uniform and El Viejo was a soldier years ago. For their sake I wish we could help, but we have barely enough for the three of us. Let the great Generalissimo Santa Anna take care of his own."

"Who are these soldiers? What are they doing on our road?" Victor was curious about this strange intrusion into their little world.

"I don't know any details, but El Viejo talked with some of them. Since he was once a soldier he knows how to talk to such men. He says Santa Anna is marching north to put down a revolt by the Texians. He says there are thousands of troops spread out across Mexico from here to Saltillo. A lot of them are hungry for fresh farm produce, so you pen the chickens and get the goats out of sight like I said before."

Victor finished his tasks and returned to his place watching the passing parade of bedraggled troops.

Two mounted soldiers stopped across the road. They talked to each other and frequently glanced in Victor's direction.

Smiling, they crossed the road to Victor. They dusted some of the gray from their red jackets and straightened their swords. Their attention was not focused entirely on Victor. His mother stood in the open door of the *caseta*; Victor was not aware of her presence, but the soldiers were.

The taller one, the one with many stripes on his sleeve, addressed his question to Victor: "You watch the soldiers with much interest, young man. Wouldn't you like to march away with them?"

Victor was too surprised to speak. Strangers seldom passed their isolated *caseta*, and here today they passed by the hundreds, perhaps by the thousands, and one had spoken to him. When he found his voice he replied, "Oh no, señor *soldado*, I have to stay here and help my mother and El Viejo take care of our garden and the animals, and it will soon be time for spring planting."

The tall cavalryman continued to smile. "Young man? How old are you?"

"I am not sure," replied Victor, but I believe I have 14 years."

The one with many stripes laughed. "Oh ho! You are joking with me! You are much too large for 14. You must have at least 16 or 17 years. Many of our soldiers have only 17 years."

Victor's mother spoke, "I assure you, *sargento,* the youngster is much too young to go marching off to war."

The soldiers looked up as though they had just discovered the mother. She was attractive but appeared aged beyond her years from exposure to the elements. The soldiers had been on the march long enough to appreciate any feminine contact beyond the camp followers that trailed the long columns: wives, mothers, sweethearts, and wagon drovers.

The tall one changed the subject. He addressed his next question to Victor, but his attention was on the mother. "Do you think your mother could spare a thirsty soldier a dipper of water?"

Victor turned to his mother. His inquisitive expression silently repeated the sergeant's question.

His mother said nothing. She walked over to the crock covered with layers of wet cloth hanging from the porch roof. She removed the gourd dipper on the side and filled it with cool water and held it out toward the dusty cavalrymen. They eased their stiff muscles out of the saddles and the tall one took the refreshment and swallowed deeply before passing it on to his partner.

"Muchas gracias, señora, that surely helps rinse away the dust of a long ride. I saw your boy there. He is certainly a fine looking lad. He seems very interested in the soldiers. The Generalissimo has authorized us to bring some new recruits into our ranks. I think the boy would make a fine soldier."

The mother answered quickly, "Oh no! It is like he says—he is much too young and we have the spring planting to do soon."

"We will be back in time for spring planting. The Texians up north are trying to revolt. All we have to do is go up with a show of force and they will go running back to their holes. They have no army or government or any kind of organization that can oppose a professional army such as ours."

"But why do you need *my* son?" You already have so many soldiers, why do you need my Victor?"

His smile had faded. "The Generalissimo has given us no choice. We are required to conscript all able-bodied males we meet on our march. Please rest assured,

señora, I will personally look after the boy and see that
no harm comes to him." He could see that she wasn't taking the news too well. "May I come inside and talk to you
privately?" He spoke aside to his partner. "Juan, you tell
the boy about the army while I speak to the señora."
The tall soldier and Victor's mother disappeared inside.

———•◦•———

Juan talked on and on about life in the army but Victor
could not have repeated any of what he said. He heard
the words but he did not put them together. He was
thinking of his mother alone in the room with the tall
stranger with stripes on his sleeves.

They emerged much later. Victor's mother avoided
looking at her son.

The tall soldier didn't. "Young man, you are going to
become a soldier in the grandest army in the world. You
will have the greatest adventure of your life. You will
earn money to buy gifts for your mother, you will make
many new friends, and you will get to wear the colorful
uniform of a soldier."

A glance at his mother told Victor that the argument
was lost. Further resistance was useless.

"Could I wear the red coat with many stripes and ride
a horse?" Victor asked.

The sergeant laughed, "Not right away, that comes
with time. You have to prove you can be a good foot soldier before you can join the cavalry. You will start with a
shiny black leather *tapa* on your head and a blue jacket
on your back. I doubt you will be in the army long
enough to wear the red jacket. Gather a few belongings—not too much, only what you can carry on your
back. We will be leaving soon. We'll give you a knapsack
for eating utensils and small items. You'll roll your
clothes in a red blanket. We'll give you one, but you may
want to bring another. The army blankets are a little
thin against these cool nights."

Victor didn't know whether to be sad or happy. He was excited about experiencing a big new adventure, but deep down his heart was heavy at the prospect of leaving all that was familiar and comfortable.

His mother spread his blanket and a few meager belongings on the table and the sergeant showed them how to roll the blanket and secure the ends. Victor did not hear the slight clink of coins in his mother's apron. She removed one of the coins and slipped it into Victor's pocket. Tears moistened both mother and son's eyes as they hugged goodbye.

"You take care, son, and come home as soon as you can. Don't worry about us. We'll do alright."

"I'll be home as soon as we finish this Texas business, Mama. I'll save my money and buy us a donkey to plow the field and carry the crop in when I get back." Victor squared his shoulders and tried to look brave as he followed the sergeant out the door. He acted more confident than he was.

Inside he was shaking.

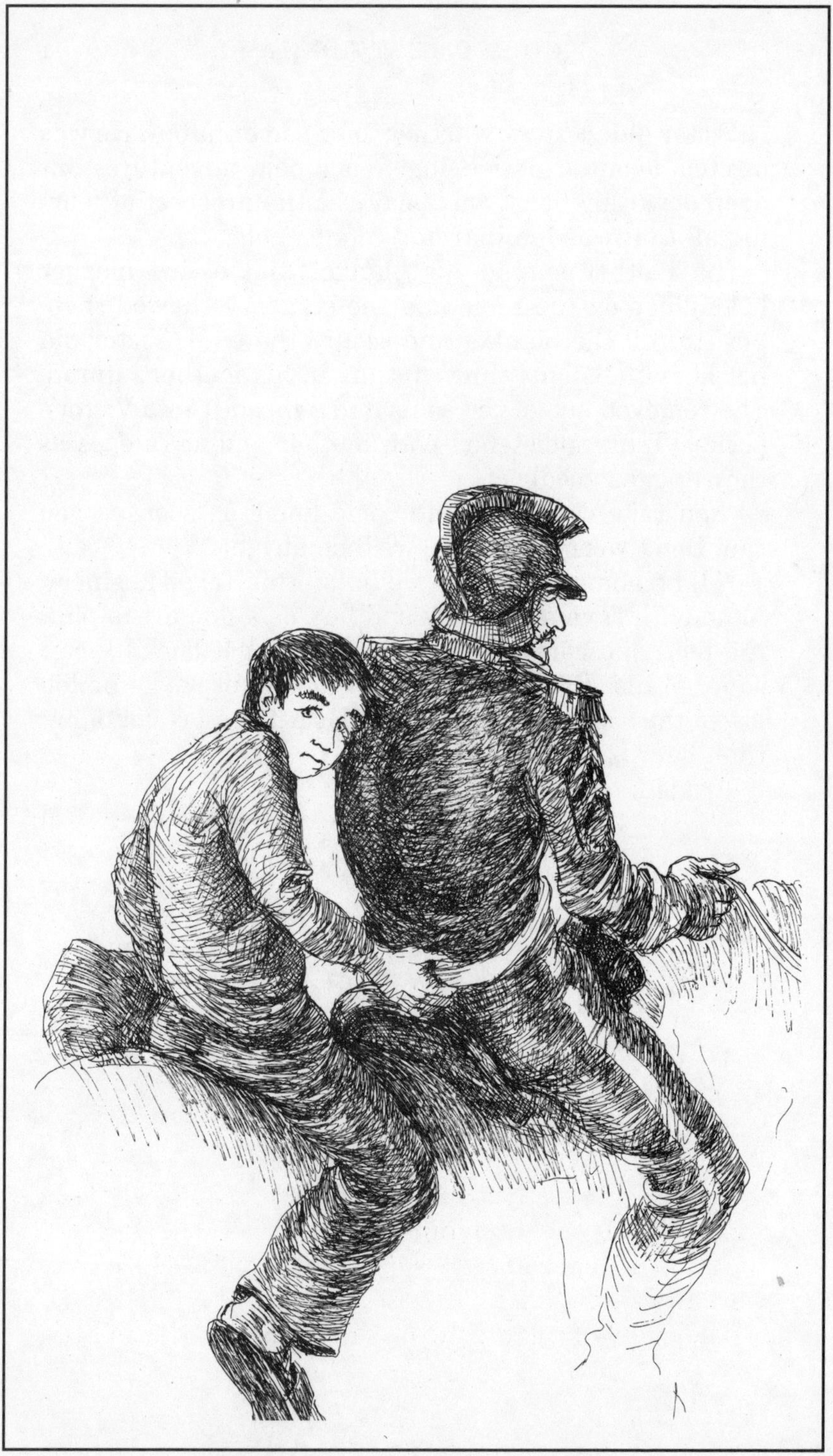

2

THE SERGEANT mounted his horse and instructed Victor to put his left foot in the stirrup. With one powerful hand, he swung the boy up behind him.

They rode silently through the shuffling ranks. When they took notice, the soldiers glanced up without interest and continued their slogging pace. The sergeant seemed to have nothing to say after leaving the little house. His jacket was not nearly so bright when seen and experienced up close. It was dirty and layered with the ever-present dust of the long march. It gave forth the combined odor of human perspiration and horse sweat. Victor was happy to take leave of his company several minutes later when they stopped at one of a group of several wagons moving at a slow walking pace alongside the marching columns of men.

The sergeant gave Victor a stirrup and helped him to the ground.

He finally spoke. "Here is the supply sergeant—he'll give you what you need for the march. If you have any questions just ask him. He's been in the army a long time. He's got all the answers. I'll see you around. Good luck and have fun."

He wheeled his horse and disappeared somewhere in the dust of the marching troops. Victor didn't see Sergeant Pena around. His only future sightings of him were from a distance.

The supply wagon pulled to a stop and a grizzly little

13

man leaped from the seat. His graying hair belied his vigor. He squinted at Victor through well-weathered, wrinkled eyelids that showed evidence of having endured many hot Mexican summers.

He spat a stream of tobacco juice in Victor's direction. The boy jerked his foot back just in time to avoid it.

"Good reflexes, son. They're sending them out younger all the time. How old are you? Oh, nevermind. You've come this far and there's no going back now. I'm Sergeant Nicolas. How are you called?"

"I am called Victor. What were you saying before about not going back?"

"You really don't know? You are in the Army of the Republic of Mexico. You are the property of Generalissimo Santa Anna until he releases you. Now back to the business of making you look like a soldier."

The nearest fit he could find was either too large or much too large. The uniform, such as it was, was not new and it had not been washed since its previous use. The jacket had a small dark-rimmed hole just over the left breast pocket. Victor shuddered and turned a few shades lighter on realizing the probable cause of the damaged jacket.

Seeing Victor's reaction, Nicolas took the garment back. "*Lo siento, muchacho*, the previous owner was very unfortunate. Here, I'll get you another." The replacement wasn't much better but at least it didn't have the bloody hole. The issue blanket was thin, dirty, and torn. Victor was glad he had his good handmade, woven blanket from home. He would put the army blanket on the ground and wrap his own around his body. He clutched his blanket tightly. It seemed to reassure him, to give him a feeling of something familiar, something from home. He was already beginning to dislike this strange new world.

Last of all the sergeant dug down in the wagon and pulled out a weapon. The gun was old, heavy, and awkward to hold. Victor pulled back the hammer and squeezed the trigger. It snapped with a solid chunk.

"Hey! Don't get in the habit of doing that! If that gun had been loaded, you'd about shot your foot off." He laughed a hollow laugh, without humor. He continued: "It's not as though you have to worry about dealing with live ammo . . . it's going to be awhile before anybody gives you ammunition to play with. For now just get used to the feel of the weapon. Somebody will be showing you how to use it soon enough."

Victor didn't like the feel of the weapon. He didn't like anything about it. His only previous contacts with any sort of weapon were his handmade slingshots made from thongs of leather and patches from old shoes. The largest game he had pursued were the rabbits that used to invade his garden. Only occasionally did he score a fatal hit to add to the dinner menu. He imagined shooting a rabbit with this new gun—it would damage the meat so that there would be little left to eat!

"Change clothes and join the march before you fall behind. It's hard to catch up you know, once you fall behind."

With no further indoctrination Victor joined in. No one seemed to notice this new addition to the ranks. It didn't take him long to realize the reason for the slow movement of the marchers.

While watching the procession earlier, he had felt he would have no problem outdistancing them in short order, but the heavy equipment and ill-fitting clothing made marching difficult. The boots rubbed blisters on his feet. The bedroll and knapsack kept shifting on his back to uncomfortable positions and he could find no way to carry the rifle that did not impede his movement. In spite of his best efforts he found himself falling behind bit by bit. When another soldier bothered to acknowledge him it was only to taunt him, to add further to his misery:

"*Qué pasa, niño?* What's the matter baby, can't you keep up?"

"Why don't you go back to the farm, little boy—
this army is for men only!"
"Your mama can't help you now, huh?"

Victor wanted to sit down, to rest if only for a few minutes, but as others continued he knew he must. His legs
seemed to move independently of his control—he had to
look down to see that they were indeed moving. There
came a point when he felt he could no longer force his
body forward. He found a bit of shade under a skimpy
mesquite bush and plopped down. He loosened his
bedroll and pack and leaned against the bundle. Every
part of his body ached. He tried to sleep but his body
hurt too much. He watched as the endless columns
passed him by. It seemed hours that he lay there. The
sun lowered toward the horizon and it seemed by this
time of day the ranks of the marchers had thinned.

He finally dozed.

"*Holà! Holà! Muchacho soldado!*"

The shouting voice brought Victor fully out of sleep.
The sun was touching the horizon and there were no
longer columns of soldiers passing by. Civilians had
replaced them. They came singly and in disorganized
groups: women and children bringing carts loaded with
personal belongings and dogs, goats, and donkeys. They
were the camp followers. If the march was difficult for
the soldiers, it must have been much more so for these
people. Their faces were dirty, worn, and hard.

The landscape was filled with these pitiful stragglers.

Victor's view of the sky was partially blocked by the
lone uniformed horseman towering above him.

"*Qué pasa?* What are you doing back here? You are
supposed to be up ahead with the rest of the soldiers."
Victor slowly sat up and rubbed his eyes.

He answered, "*Lo siento,* señor, I'm sorry. I don't think
I'm ready to be a soldier. I want to go home now. I think
I can find the way with all the tracks. The sergeant didn't
say it would be like this."

The mounted man displayed the mirthless army smile Victor had encountered so often lately.

"That sounds like Sergeant Pena. He is taking recruits much too old and much too young these days. I think he's trying too hard to make points with his superiors. It doesn't matter now though. You can't go back. The Generalissimo doesn't allow anyone to desert. If necessary he will have you chained to a wagon and dragged along."

Victor didn't recall having seen anyone chained to a wagon. The man may have been bluffing; nevertheless, he realized the mounted man meant business.

When the horse soldier spoke again his tone was softer. "The first days are always the hardest. It seems impossible now but the marching will seem easier as the days pass. You'll see."

He looked at Victor's bloody feet. The rough army boots lay nearby. Victor had replaced them with his old sandals from home.

"The boots are rubbing your feet, huh? The sandals are no solution on the long march. You need extra socks to pad the feet. Here, I have an extra pair." He took a pair of heavy socks from his saddlebag and pitched them to the boy. "Wear these as well as those you were issued. Two pair will protect your feet some."

Victor had never worn socks before. All he had worn were sandals over his bare feet. He put on both pairs and put the heavy boots back on his feet. He took up the bedroll, pack, and heavy rifle and started to walk in the direction of the marchers.

"Hold on, you'll never catch up that way. I'll give you a lift."

He dismounted and helped the boy and his cumbersome equipment onto his horse behind the saddle.

"I'll take you up to a squad of boys nearer your age. You'll find the going gets easier after awhile. I promise you. You behave now and try to keep up and I'll not tell anyone you thought of running away."

It was dark when they caught up with the main body of troops. They rode through small groups of soldiers huddled around scattered campfires. The warmth of the day vanished as the winter chill crept in.

One group of shadowy figures looked like any other to Victor as they rode on and on, but his guide seemed to know exactly where he was going. He stopped at a small camp somewhat off the main trail. One figure sat huddled over the small fire nursing a canteen cup of steaming coffee, his army blanket draped over his thin shoulders. Victor had to look close to see the other figures curled up in various positions of repose wrapped as best they could in the thin issue blankets. From what he could discern from the faces that looked up from the shadows, Victor sensed that it was a young man, a perception reinforced by the youngish voice.

"Is that you bringing in another stray, Rafael?"

"*Si*, it's me, Hector. Do you have room for *uno mas?*"

"*Si*, what's the difference, one more or one less? Tell him to get down and grab a piece of ground. There's some hot coffee and a few cold beans and tortillas left."

Victor was curious. "How do you prepare the beans so fast? At home we soak them overnight then cook them for hours after the soaking. You have only stopped a short time."

Rafael answered for the young foot soldier,"In the army we have to do it a little differently. We grind a day's supply, then dampen them a few hours before the march ends. The flavor is perhaps not so good but they cook in a very short time that way. With the addition of some spices and salt pork they are edible if you are very hungry."

The coffee was thick, black, and bitter, and the tortilla-wrapped beans were cold. It was nothing like the quality of food back home, but on this night and in these circumstances it was delicious. It had been many hours since his last meal. With his belly full he suddenly realized how tired, sleepy, and completely drained he was.

Since sundown the temperature had dropped at an accelerated rate. The chill was now penetrating. Hector and Rafael continued talking while Victor loosened his bedroll, spread the army blanket on the ground and covered himself with the blanket from home. He wrapped himself tight in its familiar textures and smells. It now seemed to be his only link to that other life he had walked away from. Could it really have been just this morning? His heart was heavy, but he was too tired to dwell on his homesickness. His fatigue quickly overcame all other considerations and he slept.

It seemed he had barely closed his eyes when Hector shook his shoulder and awakened him. There was only a hint of light on the eastern horizon to signal the approaching day.

Victor started to rise but every muscle in his body resisted.

"Move only one part at a time. Stretch your body out before you get up. You'll limber up after awhile," Hector advised.

Another voice broke in:

"I like your blanket. I would imagine you stay warm on these cold nights with such a blanket."

The speaker, to appearances, was not much older than the others in the group, and only somewhat larger, but he had a more mature muscularity. He had a primitive quality—coarseness in his demeanor and a lack of restraint. His presence was, in a word, commanding. One could sense that it could be very unwise to cross him.

Hector introduced the two: "Jose, this is Victor. He just came in last night. He'll be marching with us."

Jose's eyes did not move from Victor's blanket. "That is surely a nice blanket. I will trade you three silver pesos for it." (Three pesos represented three days' pay.)

"I'm sure it is not worth three silver coins, but I don't want to part with it. My mother and uncle made it for me and I have had it since before I can remember. It has a special meaning for me. I believe I will keep it."

"I'll give you two army blankets and the three pesos for the blanket." Jose was more demanding. He was apparently not accustomed to having someone not grant his wishes.

"No. If you already have two blankets then you don't really need mine."

Two others walked up before the conversation could go further.

"Victor, this is Ramon and Manuel. I believe they are here to tell us breakfast is ready. You and Jose can finish your bargaining later."

Breakfast was coffee, a mush made from corn meal boiled in water, a piece of salt pork, and the ever-present tortilla.

Victor learned that the small squad took turns at the cooking chores. The one whose turn it was drew rations as they were needed and cooked both meals of the day. Victor watched the others prepare their backpacks for the day's march and tried to follow suit. He recalled watching Sergeant Pena fix his pack at his family's house just the day before . . .

Hector watched his fumbling attempts. "No, no, that won't work. You'll have to roll it much tighter or the whole load will loosen and become difficult to carry." Hector showed him how to pack it right. The others largely ignored the newcomer.

Although he had no stripes on his sleeves or other marks of rank, Jose was clearly the leader of the small group. Perhaps it was his nature to lead or perhaps it was in the nature of the others to follow. Whatever the reason, he led.

"Saddle up. Let's go, boys. If we start early we can stop early and we won't have to walk quite so fast."

The sun was just beginning to show over the horizon when he stepped off. The others fell in behind in pairs, first Manuel and Ramon, then Victor and Hector. There was little conversation, as if everyone sought to conserve his energy for the upcoming day's march. The second day was every bit as hard on the body as the first, but somehow it became endurable because it was shared. When he felt he could go no farther, Victor would look around and see the others continuing and it gave him the little extra strength he needed to go on. The double layer of socks on his feet made the walking bearable.

When the sun shone straight above their heads, Jose called them to a halt. Victor saw the others chewing on something. Hector noticed his curiosity; "You didn't get your jerky ration this morning? Here, have some of mine. It's pretty awful but it eases the ache in the belly until we can stop for a real meal."

Victor took the dry, hard meat and tried to chew and swallow in a normal way. It stuck in his throat.

"You have to hold it in your mouth and chew it slowly until it softens a little. Wash it down with some water once you get it soft."

Victor did as Hector suggested. This time he managed to get some of the leathery meat down his throat.

Jose stayed a few steps ahead of the others as he set the pace. He never seemed to tire, while the others pushed to stay up.

After awhile they got into the routine of walking to the point where it became an automatic function, and talking made the going a little easier. It took his mind off of being tired. Victor told Hector of his life on the small farm and how Sergeant Pena had interrupted it. He tried to keep his voice from catching when he recounted the good times of his peaceful life.

Hector seemed to know everyone's story. "I lived in Saltillo. We were very poor and when Santa Anna came offering food, money, and adventure for the short trip north, I was one of the first men to volunteer. So far I haven't been too hungry. The food is bad but it is better then nothing, which is what I sometimes had in Saltillo. So far I haven't seen any money. Someone said we'll get some money to spend in San Antonio, but I wouldn't count on it. As for the adventure, we'll have to wait and see about that.

"Jose was with Santa Anna when he came to Saltillo. The story is he was in some battles during the revolution and he's the only one left in his squad. He doesn't talk much, but my guess is he's looking to get a squad for himself and maybe a stripe or two in the bargain. We're not far from being a squad now. Just three or four more strays and we'll be there.

"The other two, Manuel and Ramon, were picked up outside a little nameless village up the trail. They're good marchers and they do their part. They follow pretty close to Jose."

The sun was very low and small groups of soldiers had already split from the main body when Jose swung his pack down and announced, "Let's stop before it gets so dark we can't see our mouths."

Moments later all their packs were grounded. Victor's first impulse was to collapse with his pack. Jose anticipated his move:

"Hold on kid—not just yet. Everybody has to gather up a little firewood for the cooking and warming before anybody settles in. Say, I still like that blanket. Have you changed your mind about a trade?"

"Like I said before, the blanket is very special to me. It is part of my home that I left behind. I will help gather the firewood now."

The food was the same as the previous night but somewhat better for being hot. There was little talk as each person had his fill, then found a place somewhere near the fire to bundle up against the cold that crept in soon after the sun disappeared. During the busy day on the march, the body was too preoccupied with keeping up to allow the mind the luxury of reflection. Then there was no time to consider anything beyond the immediate situation. Only after he was wrapped securely in his familiar blanket could Victor allow his mind to go back—back

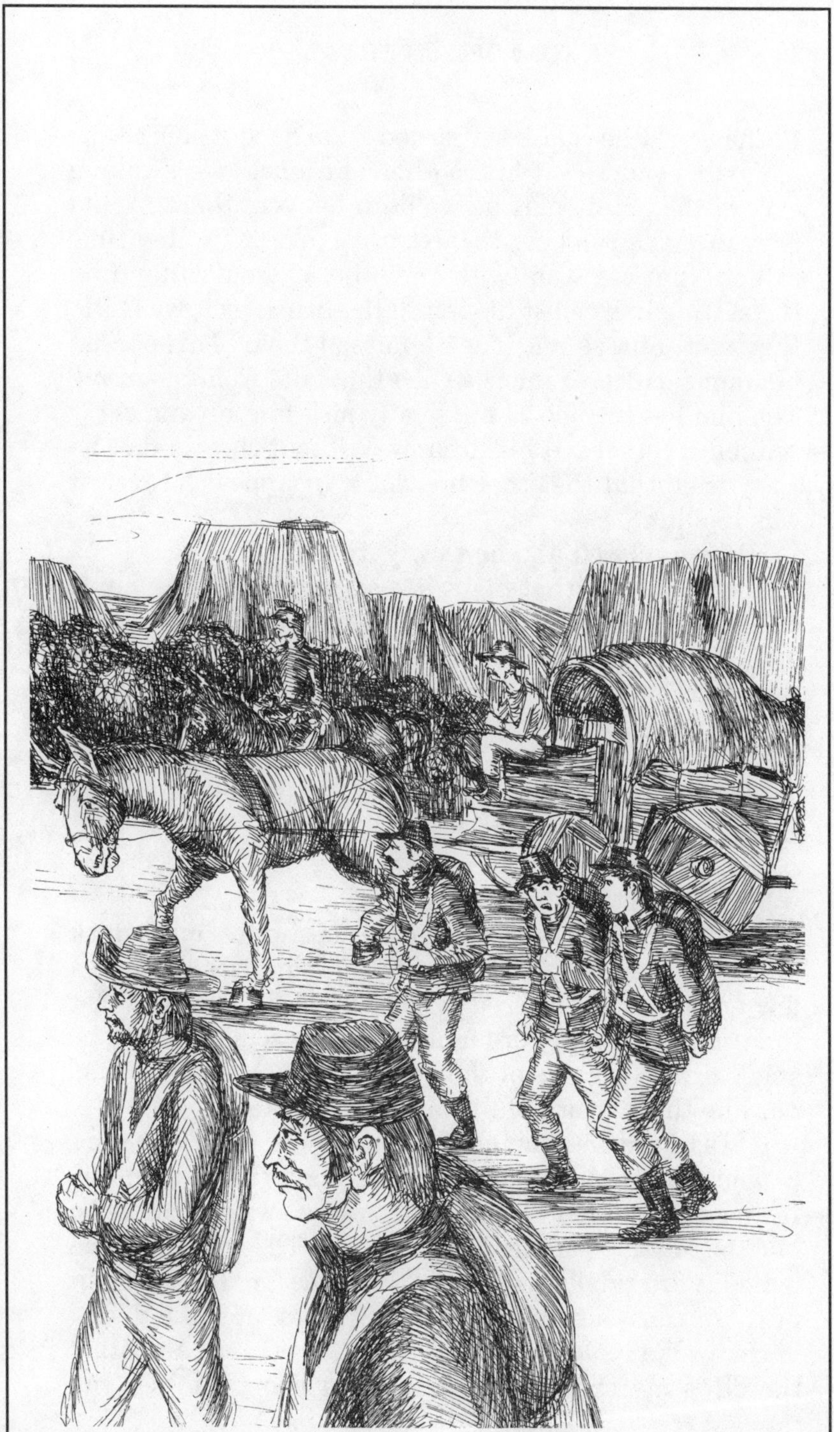

to the world he had been jerked from such a short time
ago. He wondered if his mother and uncle were taking
care of the animals as he would if he were there. Would
they give the runt pig the extra portion at feeding time
to help him catch up with the others? Would they find
the setting hen's nest hidden in the brush as it was? Did
they miss him as much as he missed them? This special
blanket seemed to release such thoughts from his mind.
The blanket seemed to physically pick him up and carry
him back. It seeded his dreams. Without the blanket he
was afraid that the other life would disappear forever. It
was his link.

His eyes closed and he slowly drifted back . . .

Sometime late that night he was aware of being much
colder. He was too tired to force himself awake, but a
deep chill gripped his body. He tried to wrap the blanket
tighter. Something was wrong. The blanket must have
slipped off sometime during the night. He reached out
for it. It wasn't there!

Maybe he had rolled over on it. Maybe it was somehow
tangled underneath him. No!

Suddenly he was fully awake.

The blanket was really missing.

The other members of his squad were only dark
bumps rising from the cold earth. The fire was down to a
few embers. He gathered some wood left over from last
night and gradually brought the dying coals to life. The
small fire took some of the edge off the chill, but it was
not like the warmth of his familiar blanket.

It was hard to imagine that one of his marching com-
panions had taken it, but that was the most likely scenario.
If that were so he'd simply have to stay awake to see who
had the missing blanket come morning. The warmth of the
building fire finally penetrated his bones and his drowsi-
ness overcame his desire to stay awake to catch the thief.

He awoke to Jose's calling them to wake up and start
the day's march. It was barely light enough to see the

bedrolls when Victor looked around. Hector's bedroll was still spread out on the ground, as was Manuel's and his own. His blanket was not among those that remained unfolded.

Jose and Ramon had already packed and rolled their blankets so it was impossible to see whether one of them had his valued possession. He was surely not going to openly accuse one of them. It was possible there was another explanation for his missing property but for the life of him he couldn't fathom what that could be. A feeling of emptiness came over him. It seemed his last full tie with home was severed with the loss of the blanket. After the usual breakfast, Jose stepped out ahead of his small group. The others fell in behind in their regular positions.

They walked quietly for awhile. Then Victor told Hector about the missing blanket.

"Maybe you can get another from the supply wagon. Jose offered to trade you two army blankets for it so he must know where there are more." Hector mouthed the words but he knew he wasn't persuading Victor. He knew Victor placed a great value on his special blanket.

"No, I want my own blanket. Did you see anyone else around our campsite last night?"

"Some things are best left alone. Why don't you get another blanket somewhere and let it drop? If you start prying you might find out more than you wish to know." Judging from the tone of Hector's voice, Victor suspected he knew more than he was telling.

"Did you see something you're not telling me about?"

"I didn't see anything for sure, but I have been here longer than you and I can guess, and what I guess is you had better let well enough alone. You have lost nothing but a blanket so far. It could be much worse," Hector was almost pleading at this point. Victor saw the futility of pushing the subject further so he let the matter drop for the time being. They continued their walk in silence.

Through the noon break Victor sat quietly chewing his jerky and observing his fellow travelers. After the earlier conversation with Hector there didn't seem to be anything left to say. Manuel and Ramon exchanged softly spoken words. Victor imagined they were talking about the small town from which they had been taken. They probably had a great deal in common with him but on this day he did not feel like making friends. Jose sat a little apart from the others. While he was not one to make light conversation, today he was particularly apart. He did not look at anyone in particular. When his eyes met another it was almost as though he were issuing a challenge. He didn't mention the blanket today. Not once did he offer a trade.

Perhaps he no longer needed to trade. He decided Jose would bear watching, but what would he do if he discovered Jose was the guilty one? How could he confront someone so much more experienced and stronger than himself? Everyone followed Jose. How would they react if there were a confrontation?

Victor sincerely hoped he was wrong in his suspicion. He was certainly no match for Jose. It never occurred to Victor to go to a higher authority. All through the remainder of the day's march and into the evening Victor didn't let his eyes leave Jose.

After supper, when everyone loosened his bedroll, there was Victor's blanket in Jose's belongings. He made no attempt to offer an explanation, like maybe he just borrowed it to try it out.

No. Nothing like that.

He spread it openly on the ground over an army blanket and looked at the others with an expression that dared anyone to offer objections. The others quickly averted their eyes as though embarrassed by what they saw. Victor was the only one who saw and continued looking.

"I believe you have my blanket!" There was sternness in his voice that surprised everyone, especially Victor.

Jose was too surprised to reply. It was the first time anyone had challenged him.

"You borrowed my blanket and now I want it back!" He was careful not to accuse the larger boy of stealing the blanket.

"It's my blanket now. I offered to get you another before and you refused. Now I'm taking this one. That is the army way. As you will learn, *muchacho*, the strong take from the weak!"

"Maybe that's your way. I don't believe it's the army way. Nothing changes the fact that it is my blanket and I want it back!"

No one was more surprised at Victor's boldness than Victor himself.

"No! That's the end of it!"

Aside, Hector pleaded with Victor. "Come on. Like he says, you'd best let this be the end of it."

Victor glared at Hector, then turned back toward Jose, who wore one of those humorless army grins that Victor had come to associate with unpleasant situations.

Suddenly, without any sort of warning, Victor swung his fist with all the strength he could muster. The blow caught Jose square on the nose, knocking him to the ground.

He sat there for several moments, too stunned to react. The blood flowed freely from his broken nose. The shock immediately turned to anger—burning, raging, terrible, vengeful anger.

He would have to crush this little creature that dared challenge his authority. He sprang to his feet and charged like a bull with lowered head and quivering muscles. Using his head for a battering ram, he would make short work of his young challenger . . .

3

INSTEAD VICTOR stepped aside and extended his foot, tripping the larger boy. Jose's face plowed into the earth. He arose more slowly this time, consumed by rage and anger, but tempered with a touch of caution. His movements were more like those of a large lumbering bear than a charging bull as he closed in on the boy.

Victor's impulse was to run for his life but he found his line of retreat cut off. The combatants were now circled by a group of onlookers attracted by the prospect of witnessing a fight. With his escape blocked, Victor chose to charge forward. This time the element of surprise was gone. Jose was ready for him. He hit Victor with a swinging right as he was coming in. A thousand stars exploded in his head and he found himself rolling on the ground, stunned. Jose rubbed his knuckles and turned to walk away, sure that the battle was over. Victor got to his knees and fell forward, grabbing both Jose's legs just below the knees, causing him to fall. Before Jose could rise, Victor was straddling his body, pounding on his chest. In Jose's opinion, this wasn't supposed to be happening. He rolled over and tumbled Victor from his position of advantage. Victor jumped to his feet and kicked Jose in the chest. Victor knew none of the finer aspects of fighting; this was the first time he had struck or had been struck by another human being.

Jose was by now finding himself in a no-win situation. A quick conclusion would be interpreted as a simple disciplinary action in which an enlisted man is put in his place in short order. An extended conflict would be a bully punishing a youngster beyond acceptable limits. If, by some lucky quirk, the boy won over the more powerful opponent, then Jose would lose face. He could never hope to gain the respect necessary for a leader.

For several seconds the two battled toe to toe, exchanging punches with neither giving ground. Soon though, the greater size and strength of Jose began taking its toll. Victor had to cover up and step back. Jose charged in with renewed vigor, raining blow after blow on his weakening victim. Another solid punch to the midsection sent Victor to his knees again. He gasped for breath that was not there. He managed to grasp Jose around the waist and pulled him to the ground. Jose grabbed both Victor's arms in a powerful bear hug. He held tight and the action paused as both caught their breath. Jose put his mouth close to Victor's ear and spoke softly so as not to be overheard by the bystanders, "Come on now kid, you've put up a good fight. I'll hit you one more light punch and you can go down with honor."

"Will you return my blanket?"

"You know I can't do that. I would lose face. A leader can't lose face. Come on now, let me tap you and you can still have the respect of one who has put up a good fight."

Jose released his grip, hoping Victor was prepared to accept his offer and go down, letting them both quit the field without loss of face. Victor twisted loose and stumbled to his feet, assuming a fighting pose. Jose tapped him lightly on the jaw, making a slap look like a solid blow. He stepped back to give Victor a chance to go down and end the fracas. Instead of going down, Victor stepped forward and gave Jose a punch every bit as hard as that first one and in the same place, the freshly broken, very sensitive nose. The pain exploded through Jose's head. He had just given this beaten kid a chance at mercy, a chance to go down mostly intact and emerge with honor, but the ungrateful whelp had the audacity to renew a fight he knew he could not win. Now there could be no mercy.

Jose shrieked his rage and charged again with the fury of a large wounded jungle beast. He pulled no punches as he put his full strength into each blow. Repeatedly Victor was knocked to the ground only to rise again, each time more slowly than the times before. The onlookers were no longer watching a sporting event. It had degenerated into carnage. They alternately called for Jose to stop and for Victor to lay down. Victor was no longer exchanging blow for blow. His punches, when landed, were weak, feeble taps that did no damage. Jose's blows had not weakened. They were powerful and devastating. Some of the spectators turned away, sickened by the cruelty.

Then, after a particularly punishing barrage, Victor did not get up.

He lay very still.

The fight was over.

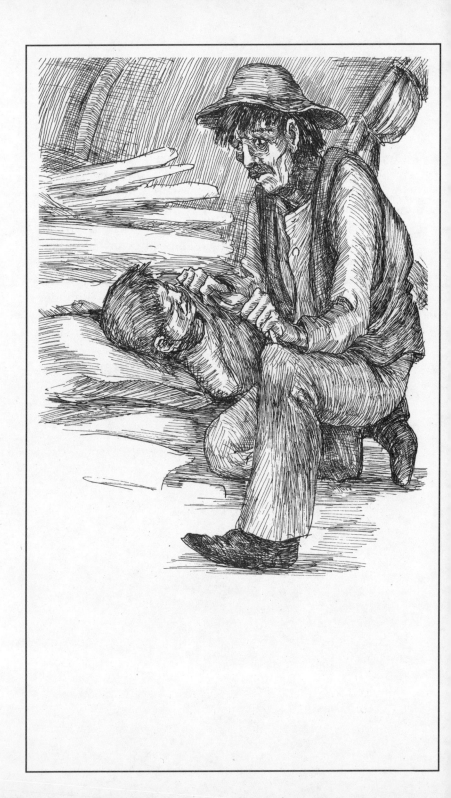

4

"Oh, you're not dead after all. I was beginning to wonder if you'd ever come around."

Victor opened his eyes to see an ancient, lined face looking down at him. The canvas roof, stacked uniforms, and other army gear told him that he was lying in a supply wagon.

He was wrapped in his familiar blanket from home.

Maybe this whole experience had been a terrible nightmare.

He tried to sit up; pain from most of his joints and all his muscles told him it had been no dream. He raised a bandaged hand to his aching face. It was bruised, cut, and swollen from the fight.

"If you think it's bad now, you should have seen it yesterday right after the fight." The voice was soft but strong, like that of a much younger man.

"Yesterday! What happened to the time between? I can't remember." The words came with great effort through swollen lips. Every movement of the jaw was accompanied by sharp pain.

"Don't try to talk too much just yet. The big boy beat you up pretty bad. We thought you were dead but I saw the breath was still coming, although slow. I washed you up and felt for broken bones. You are still in one piece I think, but you aren't ready to walk yet. Lay still and enjoy the free ride. You'll be on the march soon enough. I have some medicine that will help you rest." He gave Victor a generous swallow of laudanum. The bitter taste passed quickly in favor of the soothing effects of the powerful sedative. Victor leaned back and gave in to the drug. He slipped in and out of consciousness over the course of the next several hours.

He awoke again, feeling much better. He moved up to the driver's seat beside the old soldier.

"Muchas gracias, señor, I believe I owe you much for picking me up and nursing me back."

"*De nada, muchacho.* There are others who would have done the same. I heard the others call you Victor. If we are to travel together for awhile we should know each other's name. They call me Pedro here. When I marched with Napoleon some twenty or so years ago, they called me Pierre to fit in with the French. I was just a boy then, not much older than you. I think sometimes that Generalissimo Santa Anna believes he is Napoleon, come back to fight again! In some ways they are alike, but I am afraid our Santa Anna has not the consistency of the Frenchman, and he doesn't care so much for his men. Someday that will be his downfall."

"How did you come from Napoleon to Mexico?" Victor used his words sparingly. His jaw was still sore. The old man didn't need encouragement. He liked to talk about the old times.

"When an army is defeated it is not wise to stay around if an opportunity comes to move on. Sometimes the winner thinks only of revenge and punishment for the conquered ones. My dark complexion and knowledge of the language made it easy for me to find a place in the Spanish army. The life of a soldier is all I have ever known. We were shipped to Mexico to settle the uprisings there. I changed sides from time to time to stay alive. I wasn't sure which side was right and which was wrong or what each side was fighting for. In the skirmishes that followed over the years, my body stopped a few bullets. I'm tough . . . too tough to be stopped by a few bullets, but each one slowed me down a little. Now I'm slowed down close to a full stop. I don't sit a horse very well anymore and my legs are too shot up to make the long marches now. This may be my last campaign. It's even getting hard to sit a wagon anymore . . . "

Pedro had a never-ending supply of war stories. He entertained both himself and Victor. He talked for two days straight without repetition.

Between the stories and the medicine, Victor was beginning to enjoy the army experience. The days were passing much easier away from the march.

One day a cavalry sergeant approached the wagon. His comments suggested he was familiar with the last few days' events: "*Muchacho,* you are looking much healthier now. I think you had better get used to walking again. Walk beside the wagon for awhile and as soon as you are feeling strong enough you need to rejoin your old squad."

Victor felt strong as ever, barring a few old lingering aches and pains but he wasn't particularly anxious to give up his free ride to return to the grueling march. Not the least of his concerns was how the others would receive him. Would Jose try to continue to extract vengeance? Would the others bear ill feeling toward him for attacking their leader? How and why had his blanket been returned? Who was responsible? Would he still be able to bear up under the marching regime?

He was comfortable riding on the wagon with the old soldier, listening to his stories, and sleeping on a soft surface wrapped in his familiar blanket every night.

Such was not to continue.

A couple of days later, the sergeant was back to take Victor to his unit. Victor had no idea which direction to go in.

He asked the sergeant, "Am I going to be in trouble for fighting our squad leader?"

"I wouldn't worry too much about that. Your private Jose has no stripes. It is not like you struck an officer.

After the scrap you put up, I don't think he'll be so anxious to tangle with you again. You marked him for life with that nose job you know."

"Who returned my blanket?"

"Blanket? Oh yes, that's what started it, *si?*" No one knows for sure. I suspect it was Jose himself, but he wouldn't admit it. I wouldn't press him about it."

Victor need not have worried about being reunited with his squad.

"*Holà, mi compadre!* How are you doing?" It was Jose. He came forward with his hand extended in greeting. "It's good to have you back."

The three who had been in the squad previously joined Jose in his greeting.

The squad had picked up additional recruits during Victor's absence. There were three more Mexicans and two Yucatec Indians added to the group. Jose still acted as leader but he hadn't been given any stripes to go with his authority. He had thought that as soon as his unit came up to strength the stripes would be forthcoming. They weren't. The three Mexicans, all youngsters, had been conscripted off their farms, much like Victor. The Indians had been brought in from another group out of a large number that were dragged in from somewhere below Saltillo. Their status was near slavery. They entered the army in chains, without uniforms or provisions. They didn't even know the language. Victor felt for them but there was little he could do to make their lot any easier.

Jose did a one-sided introduction to the newcomers. Perhaps he had forgotten the names of the Mexican recruits; the two Indians' names he had never known. "I want you to meet the best fighter in the Mexican army, next to me. My good friend, Victor!"

The five newcomers were reserved in their greeting.

There was no significant news beyond what the sergeant had told him on the way over, but he sat and listened to the retelling anyway.

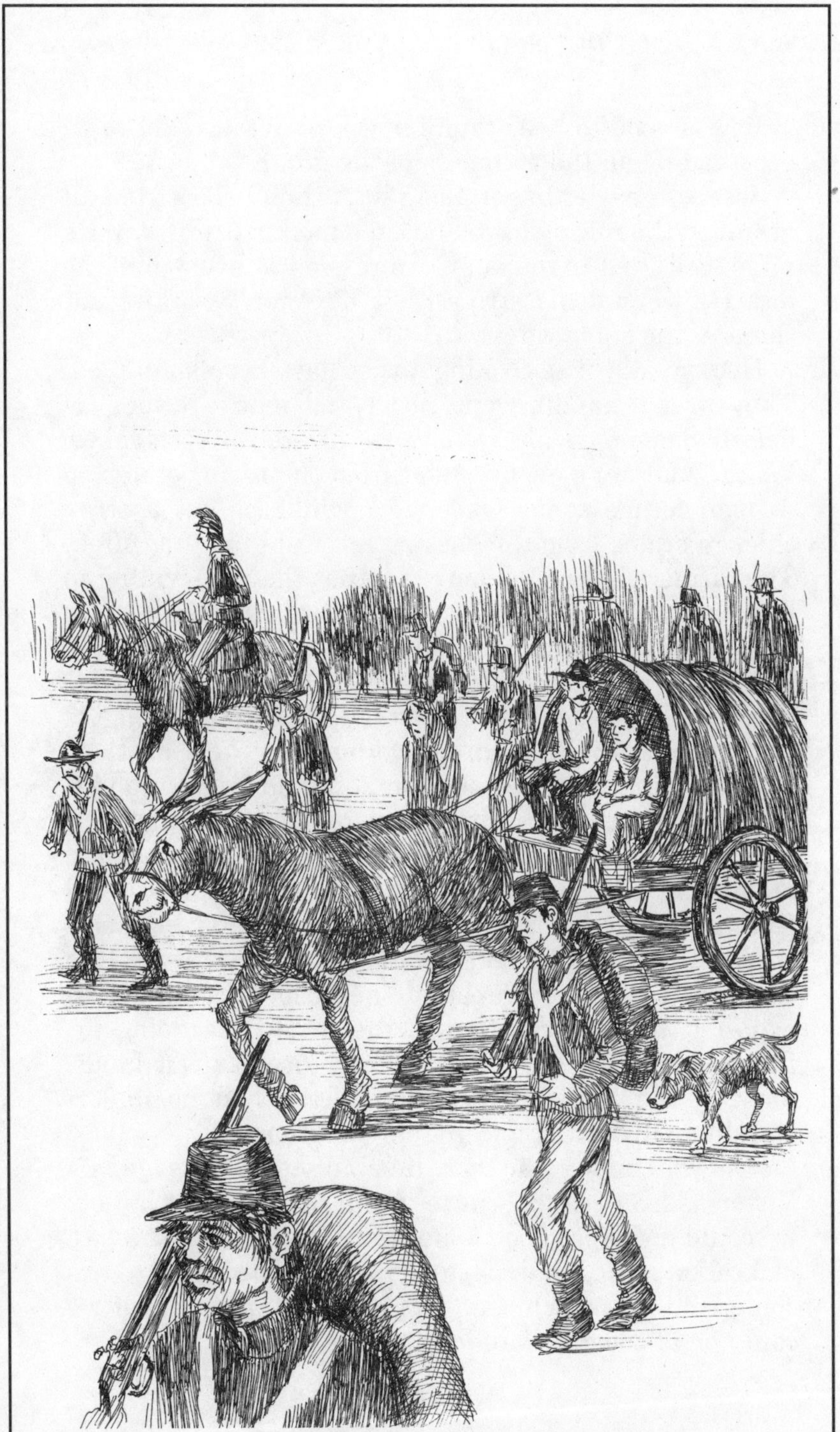

It was good to hear familiar voices and a relief to be accepted by all the members of the group.

Jose was easier to get along with than before. He still assumed the role of leader, but in a more natural way. He no longer tried to make an impression in everything he did. He wanted his stripes, but he wasn't working for them in the same way.

Hector said, "The cooking duties have been simplified. They aren't handing out nearly as many rations as before. Some days all we have to eat are the corn cakes. We are marching even farther from the main column so we can forage some. Once in a while we get a stray chicken or dog from the passing farms, but not too often. The farmers are not so patriotic that they are willing to feed Santa Anna's army and go hungry themselves. We do better than many units. Jose knew some of the supply sergeants from before, so sometimes they give him a little extra, like the blankets for the Indians. They came to us with only the thin cotton clothes they wore on their backs. Jose acquired some blankets and basic supplies for them. That's more than most squads are doing."

Victor sympathized with the farmers along the route for having been one himself, but he didn't express his feelings openly. He knew the others were in favor of satisfying their own hunger before concerning themselves with the plights of strangers. The farmers could not be expected to appreciate what the army was doing for them in chasing the Texians from the Mexican lands. Most of the soldiers, including Victor, had no understanding of what they were marching for.

"Do you know who has the bullets for the guns?" Victor asked of no one in particular. "If we had bullets we could perhaps shoot some game. Yesterday I saw two jackrabbits and some days ago I saw a deer. There are some wild prairie chickens and turkeys out there if we could be allowed to wander far enough to find them."

Jose answered, "The army isn't about to let you squander their ammunition on anything as frivolous as food. You'll be lucky if they give you bullets to shoot at the enemy."

Something occurred to Victor. He made a strange-sounding request to Jose: "Have the boys watch out for discarded shoes or boots. If you find some, bring them to me. I have an idea."

"What can you do with old boots and shoes? By the time this army discards footwear it is beyond any reasonable use. If you have a mind to cook them up, they are too tough, and I doubt there's any nourishment there. Besides, you'd never get rid of the odor."

Victor laughed, "Oh no, it's nothing like that. Just get me some old shoes and I'll show you!"

"I think maybe I knocked some of your brains loose, but out of curiosity I'll get you old shoes and we'll see. I hope you aren't trying to make the joke on me."

"No, I wouldn't do that. Bring me the old shoes and you'll see."

By the end of the next march, Victor had an assortment of worn out shoes and boots. They looked beyond redemption, but Victor inspected each one as thought he was looking for something special. At last he selected a few, but he still wouldn't reveal his plans to the others. He had their full attention as they watched his every move. There was some suspicion that he had indeed lost his mind, but he was so intent on his task that they knew something was stirring. Victor took a well-worn jackknife from his pocket and carved a large oval shape out of a soft piece of undamaged leather. He went through the entire collection of footwear and removed all the leather tie strings. He discarded those that were knotted or worn too thin. The remainder he tested for strength and kept the two best. He punched holes in the ends of the oval and tied one of the leather thongs to either end. He smiled and held up his handiwork for everyone to admire.

All he got were puzzled expressions.

He had confirmed their suspicions that he was indeed losing his mind. They turned to walk away.

He called them back. "Haven't you heard the story of David and Goliath?" His mother had told him the story many times, and his uncle had shown him how to make a slingshot like David's. He would tell the story later—now a demonstration was called for!

"Look. See that cactus over there? Watch it."

He took a rounded rock about half the size of his fist and placed it in the oval piece of leather between the thongs. He held the ends of the thongs in his hand and started a large swinging motion. Faster and faster it whirled until it sang in the air. When it was a blur of movement he released one end of the thong at a practiced moment. The stone hit the cactus with a smashing blow that sent bits of the cactus flying for yards around. It wasn't exactly the part of the cactus Victor had been aiming for, but the others didn't know the difference.

Astonishment showed in the faces of all the onlookers.

"Now who needs bullets for the old rifles? Just show me a rabbit or a prairie chicken and I'll show you a good meal with meat!"

After the demonstration everyone wanted to have one of the new contraptions. With Victor's help they made two more from the supply of old footwear. Jose and Hector took immediate control of those. Victor kept the first and best for himself.

For the next few days it wasn't safe to be within range of those three slingshots. They knocked the tops off a few cactus plants, scared away most of the potential game, and had a few soldiers ducking from time to time, but they didn't add to the menu.

Victor finally succeeded in bringing down a prairie chicken. The small nibble of meat only served to whet their appetites and encourage them to continue practicing

with the new toys. The slingshots gave them some diver-
sion from the long march. It took their minds off their
troubles to some degree, but they would require more
practice before their slingshots would become effective
hunting tools.

As if the low food supply wasn't bad enough, a water
shortage developed. When they did find water, it was
muddy or rancid, but the marchers drank it in despera-
tion. Many became ill and some cattle died of thirst. Jose
had his group boil any doubtful water before drinking it,
so his squad was spared the illness that befell others.

"We will be in Laredo in a day or two. We should be
able to re-supply there. Everybody is ready for some real
food. If we have to go much farther like this, people will
be dying of hunger," Jose announced to the group.

But Laredo proved a disappointment. Most of the
townspeople had evacuated in anticipation of the arriving
soldiers. They had taken with them all the personal
belongings they could carry. Nevertheless, the army
looted whatever remained—everything else that was
portable and held any value. Officers found a few stores
of grain and some livestock. They left chits promising
payment for the appropriated goods. The chits were
worthless, of course. Santa Anna didn't have the funds to
pay his own army, much less the civilians.

From their position at the edge of the main column,
Jose and his squad saw very few civilians.

Jose disappeared one evening with Manuel and
Ramon. They returned a few hours later with burlap
bags loaded with food and some basic goods. Victor and
Hector were not inclined to question the source of their
good fortune. The others followed their example. They
would be well fed for a few days at least.

The pause at Laredo ended all too soon. The grueling
march resumed.

Two days north of Laredo brought the rabbits, thousands of them!

The previous week's practice with the slingshots was

well rewarded. There was rabbit stew, fried rabbit, roasted rabbit, and rabbit prepared in every conceivable way.

Where did all the rabbits come from? There were more rabbits than any of them had ever seen in their lives.

"What are you doing?" Jose asked of the three Mexican recruits who were on their knees mumbling and making the sign of the cross.

"We are giving thanks to the Holy Mother for our great good fortune. We were starving and now She has provided us with an abundance of food."

"I would not be so quick to celebrate our good fortune. I've noticed that when things get too good, something bad is about to happen."

It made Victor uneasy when someone made light of another's religious practices. All the same, he would withhold his thanksgiving until the end of their adventure.

Jose was bothered by anything that didn't make sense to him. He refused to accept supernatural intervention as an explanation.

Something was not right. He could feel it in the air. Jackrabbits do not suddenly go against their nature and start traveling in herds. Maybe four or five together at one time at most, but not by the hundreds! This was just not natural and it bothered him.

He looked toward the north to see a darkening ridge very low on the horizon. It extended all across the northern sky, and affected only that part of the sky. The rest was still light blue and clear. Such things were not common deep in Mexico from where most of the young men had come.

A blue Texas norther!

It can come without warning and in less than a quarter-hour it can lower the temperature by forty degrees or more. The wind, sometimes blowing fifty miles an hour, pushes the cold through anything in its path. Creatures exposed to its fury can be dead in a very short time. Wild animals can sense an oncoming norther and seek shelter or try to outrun it. On this day, thousands of jackrabbits

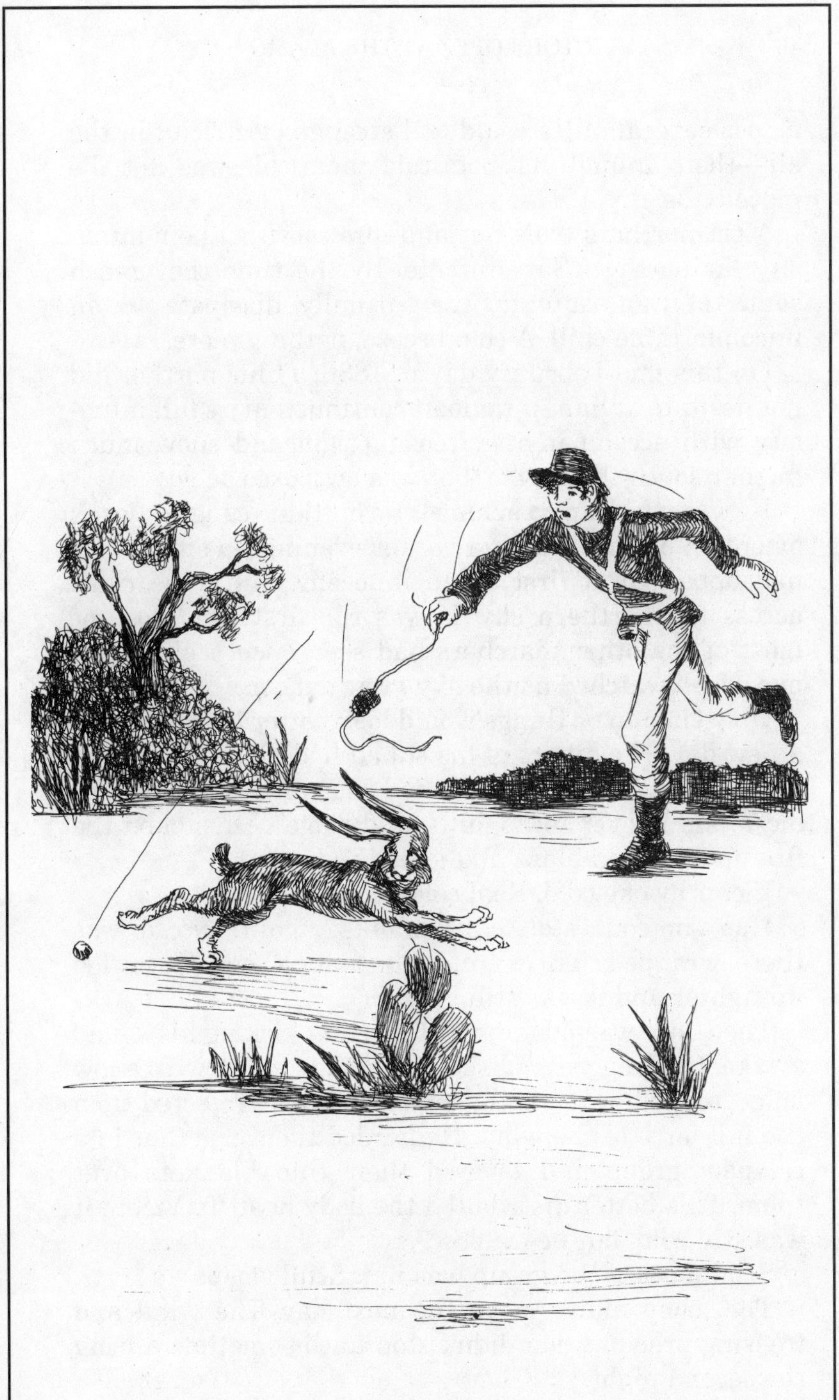

across several miles could feel strange electricity in the
air—their animal instincts told them this was not the
place to be.

Most northers blow out and lose most of their intensity far north of San Antonio. By the time they reach
south of San Antonio, they usually dissipate to an
uncomfortable chill. A cold breeze, nothing more.

On this mid-February day in 1836, a blue norther did
not hesitate at San Antonio. It continued in its full intensity with accompanying freezing rain and snow much
farther south than a norther was supposed to go.

It was this approaching storm that caught Jose's
attention on this cool mid-winter evening—a storm that
had appeared at first as an innocent, thin, blue ridge
across the northern sky. It was the first time Jose or
most of the other marchers had seen such a phenome-
non. They watched as the sky grew darker.

Oh well, maybe things would look better in the light of
a new day. The others of his squad had already bundled
up early for a night's rest. It had been an especially hard
day's march over rocks, hills, and ridges. He stoked the
fire up to a good blaze and joined them.

Victor awoke cold. Real cold . . .

Had someone stolen his blanket again? No, it was
there, wrapped tightly around his entire body. He curled
up tighter and it was still cold.

Then Jose was pushing, yelling, and kicking his squad
awake. He dragged and shoved them one by one to a low
ledge, topped by a small clump of bushes protected from
the full force of the wind. He herded them together in a
compact group and layered their thin blankets over
them. This better distributed the body heat. To Victor, it
was still cold, but bearable.

Soon most of the group was in a fitful sleep.

The army didn't move the next day. The wind and
freezing precipitation didn't stop until sometime during
the second night.

The next morning was quiet. Erie, silent mounds of ghostly white snow took form in the increasing morning light; white mounds that had not been there before the storm.

Curious, Victor went to one of the nearer mounds and dusted some snow away to see what had caused the unusual change in the landscape. He recoiled in horror.

A frozen face stared back at him through the snow. Others of his group were making similar discoveries. Bodies of men and animals were scattered where they had fallen, in their tracks, to freeze to death and be buried under a shroud of ice and snow. Most of those frozen bodies were Indians who had been conscripted into the army without proper clothing for the cold. Coming from southern Mexico, they had never experienced cold weather, much less snow and freezing rain.

Their Indians were among the lucky survivors, thanks to Jose's bunching them up.

No one spoke during breakfast. Each person tried to avoid looking up at the many white mounds of snow covering their grotesque parcels. They hurried to pack and be on their way, away from those grizzly mounds.

A few vultures circled slowly overhead, patiently waiting for the living to move on so they could pick the bones of the dead.

Other scavengers preyed closer to earth. Skulking figures darted from one mound to another, brushing off snow and stripping the corpses of anything of value. The pickings were very slim from the fallen Indians and only somewhat better off the Mexican soldiers—a pair of boots here, a weapon there, and a few worn blankets.

Victor wondered about these two-legged, earthbound scavengers. "Jose, who are these creatures who go about picking the dead?"

"I was curious about that myself. I asked one of General Cos' sergeants about that. His troops were here before and the Texians chased them back to Mexico.

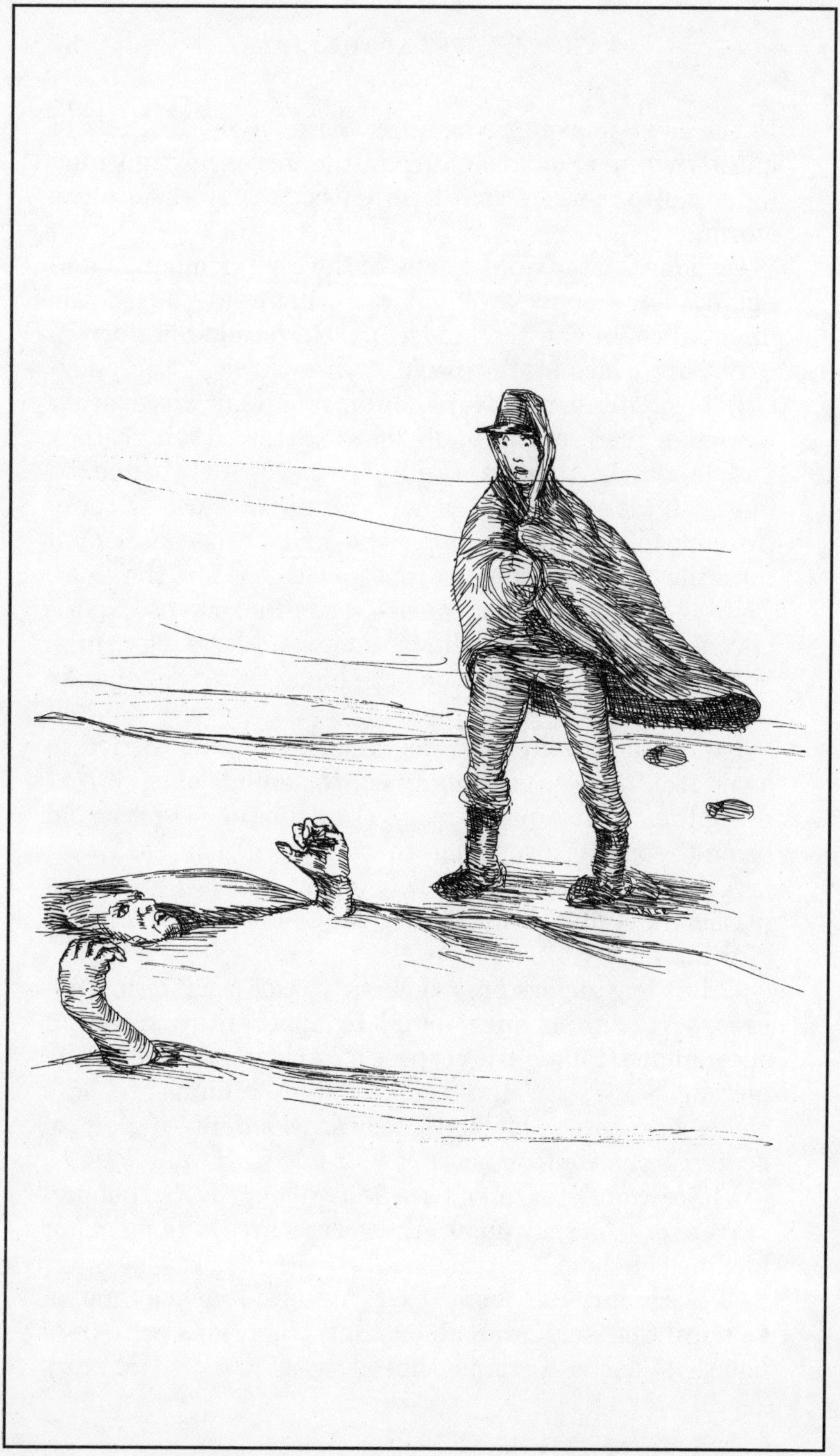

Those body pickers are Indians, but not like the Indians marching with us. These are Lippon Apaches.

"They are used to this changing Texas weather. They wear clothing made from animal skins and blankets. We are seeing a few women, children, and old men. If you encounter a few isolated Indians like these, they are fairly harmless. Winters are hard on them and sometimes they get pretty desperate. Don't let these fool you. Their warriors are fierce fighters when several of them get together for a war party. This is not their main hunting ground. They usually range farther west nearer the mountains.

"What you have to look out for in this part of the country are the Comanches: they are nothing but mean. If they had any kind of organization they'd wipe us all out. They won't attack a full-size combat unit above company strength, but if they catch a few soldiers away from the main body, watch out!"

"How can you tell the difference between one kind of Indian and another?"

"You can't, really. On foot they look a lot alike. There are those who can look at their clothes and weapons and tools and tell, but I can't. We think of the Comanches as being much taller because they're nearly always seen on horseback. The Apaches ride horses, of course, but not like the Comanches. They're the best horsemen in the world, bar none, those Comanches. I guess the difference is the Apaches are mostly mountain Indians and the Comanches are mainly plains Indians."

Victor was relieved when the marching progress placed them out of the area marked by the white mounds and scavenging Apaches.

It was still cold but the biting edge was gone. It left when the wind died down. The ice and snow melted rapidly under the rising sun. After the early morning, stiffness left their bodies and the marching was easier. The cold seemed to spur them on to greater speeds. The ranks didn't really appear thinner, despite the loss of the soldiers who had frozen to death. There were still countless soldiers plodding along as far as the eye could see, fore and aft.

The day passed quickly and the sun was low when Victor spotted a fat calf, several months old, just off the trail. It was bawling as loud as it could, obviously separated from its mother. It seemed to be caught in some brush.

Victor yelled at the others, "Hey, come here! I think I've just found our supper! Help me catch him!"

The others responded faster than you could tell about it. They hit the bush holding the calf all at once. Hector wrapped his hands around its neck while Ramon and Manuel both grabbed a leg. Victor made a dive at the body and missed. He didn't secure a hold on the calf but succeeded in knocking the grips of the others loose, freeing the calf from the bush.

"Come on boys, we can still catch him! There's just one of him and ten of us. Let's go!"

Jose made a running jump and landed on the back of the frightened calf. The added weight slowed the calf, but didn't stop it by any means. One of the Indians caught a handful of tail. Just as the others came up, Jose fell off and the Indian lost his hold. The calf broke loose, ran a few steps, and stopped.

Victor had had a little experience chasing loose stock. "Hold it boys. Let's surround him slow and easy then close in real quiet so we don't spook him."

The calf stood still for several moments, trying to catch its breath. The boys formed a large circle around their quarry, but before they could close in the calf bolted again. This time it ran a good fifty yards out before it stopped, as if daring his pursuers to continue the chase.

There was no giving up now. They could taste the feast of fresh roast beef the fatted calf would provide.

This time they spread out and moved in very slow. They had almost closed in when the calf broke loose again. They tried the maneuver several more times without success, each time putting more distance between

them and the main body of troops, who at this point were
about a half-mile away.

They finally cornered the calf against the bank of a
curving *arroyo* and ganged up on it.

Jose ended its short life with a quick slash of his knife
across the throat.

"We won't have to skin it out all the way. We'll just
take the hindquarters. They should dress out pretty fast.
This is sure gonna beat that diet of jackrabbit and
prairie chicken."

With a practiced hand, Jose cut off the hindquarters
and pulled the skin loose.

"Manuel and Ramon, you're the best cooks, you roast
it up and get the Indians and recruits to gather some
wood while me and Victor and Hector go back for the
packs. We'll camp after we eat."

They were in good humor going back to the starting
point of the chase.

"We went a good piece out of the way chasing that crit-
ter. I didn't realize we'd gone so far." It was clear that
Jose was annoyed.

"Maybe we should have just carried the beef over
here," Hector said.

"I guess I was so anxious to get the meat cooking . . .
that was the main thing on my mind at the time. It did-
n't seem so far when we were running all excited-like,
chasing that dumb calf. If our foresight was as good as
our hindsight, we'd all be considerably smarter. We may
as well make the best of it now."

The others laughed at Victor's next comment. "With
this experience maybe we'd do well to plan to pool our
money for some cattle and become vaqueros when we get
out of the army."

"Who wants to get out of the army anyway? We have
plenty of good food, the fun of the march every day, and
we'll all be rich as soon as they pay us." Hector's state-
ment, delivered in his dry, matter-of-fact way, got a bigger
chuckle than Victor's did.

Jose, turning serious, added, "You know, that cowboy idea wasn't so bad. After we chase those Texians back to wherever they came from, there's gonna be a whole lot of land up there, and I figure the veterans of Santa Anna's army might have first choice. There are cattle out there for the taking. That's something to think about, just the three of us living off the land."

Victor wondered just how much land Santa Anna would allot to each veteran of the conflict to put down the rebellion. He didn't see himself working the soil as a dirt farmer. He didn't mind working the soil on a small scale, like at home where they only grew enough for their meager needs. But his aspiration was to work with large numbers of cattle from horseback, like the fathers did at the missions he had heard of. It would be such great fun riding a horse all day every day. He would likely require a large volume of land to fulfill his plans. Such land would likely be possible only if he and his comrades combined their land grants. He heard that cattle ran wild and free for the taking. Working together they could build an empire. His dreams were high. With sufficient effort there was no limit to what they could do. Cattle, horses, and more . . . it would be a great adventure.

Hector picked up on the idea. Excitement was in his voice. "Say, that would really give us something to look forward to. It can't be too hard to learn how to herd cows if you have a good horse."

None of them knew what was really involved in being a cattleman, but in talking about it they were all three enthused with the idea of becoming vaqueros. That was all they could talk about the rest of the walk. None of them so much as noticed the double and triple weights of their packs on the way back to the new campsite.

The odor of roasting beef urged them on toward their destination . . .

There was plenty for all and some leftovers for the coyotes when the boys finished gorging themselves.

They sat around the campfire, warm and drowsy with

full bellies. The fire was built under the protective ledge in the bend of the *arroyo* where the calf was caught. The ledge served as a windbreak. Although the norther had mostly blown itself out, there was still a significant breeze and the temperature dropped sharply after sunset. As the fire died away the comfortable troopers bundled up and were soon asleep.

Victor was awake before the first light, aroused by the call of a whippoorwill nearby. The call of the whippoorwill is not an intrusive sound to someone who is half-asleep, but something about this whippoorwill call was different, and disturbing. Then there was another call some distance from the first, then yet a third. They seemed to be calling back and forth to each other.

Suddenly something grasped Victor by the arm. Before he could cry out another hand closed over his mouth. Then there was a voice very close to his ear.

"Do you hear those birds? The whippoorwills are sounding very peculiar this morning, don't you think? Carefully and quietly now let's awaken the others. Stay low and pretend to be asleep, but stay alert."

"*Qué pasa?* What's happening?" Hector exclaimed when Victor shook him awake.

"Shhh! Comanches!"

5

THE OTHERS WERE aroused one by one with a minimum of disturbance.

Every sound was magnified in their imaginations. All conversation was in whispers.

"They've got us cut off out here. We have no defense except these guns with no ammunition! We can fix the bayonets, but they have spears, tomahawks, and bows with arrows . . . we'd never get close enough to use bayonets. Worst of all they have horses if they're Comanches. We might bluff them for awhile, but they'll learn soon enough that the guns won't shoot."

"How many do you suppose are out there?"

"Probably not too many. It's most likely a small war party out to pick off any stragglers that get separated from the main group. Small groups like us. We need to find a way back to the rest of the marchers or somehow get word to them that we're out here in need of help . . . "

"We're in a more or less protected spot here. If we all run for it they can cut us to pieces in the open," Victor reasoned.

"I think our best chance," decided Jose, "is to have one man slip through and go for help. It can't be much more than a half-mile back to the marchers. If somebody goes it will have to be real soon before it gets too light. I'm the toughest one here. I don't think anyone here can argue that. I'll be the . . . "

"Everyone knows you're tough," Manuel interrupted, "but what's important now is speed, and everyone here

knows I'm fast—faster than you. I can find my way there
and be back with help in less time than it takes to stand
here and talk about it."

Before anyone could say anything further or make a
move to stop him, Manuel was gone.

Manuel was several yards away snaking his way
through the scant cover of scattered bushes, before the
realization struck him: what had he gotten himself into?
If he moved fast enough he would make it. It was still
the darkness before first light; details of the landscape
were lost in the shadows. Any shadow could be an Indian
or hopefully just another bush or rocky outcropping. He
couldn't pause to investigate. He had to move fast. In a
matter of moments, those objects in the shadows would
become visible. As they became visible, he would become
visible. So he moved as quickly and quietly as possible.
The light was increasing by the second. He hadn't seen
any Indians yet. Maybe it was only whippoorwills they
had heard earlier. Maybe there were no Indians at all.
Only moments more and he would reach the main column. There now, just ahead, the shadowy figure of a cavalryman riding tall in the saddle, his plume adding to his
height.

Manuel stood up and shouted, *"Holà hay soldada!
Venga aquí!"*

The horseman moved closer, his plume waving in the
breeze. Cavalrymen's plumes are stationary—they do
not move in the breeze . . .

Those were feathers! He had waved and shouted to an
Indian. If he had continued as he was going he might
have passed unseen to the soldiers. Now that line of
travel was blocked. He turned to run back to where he
had come from. Suddenly that way was blocked by
another Indian, and yet another and another. He had left

his rifle because it weighed too much. As if it would have helped with no ammunition . . .

He would go down fighting.

He pulled his bayonet from his belt and charged toward the nearest Indian, shouting at the top of his lungs. Before he could reach the horseman he felt a sharp pain in his back, followed by another. The pain increased and he felt himself falling through space. His arms and legs didn't seem to function anymore.

Back at the campsite, the others waited for Manuel to return. The strange whippoorwills stopped. It grew very quiet. Then, in the distance, the faint sound of Manuel's voice hailing the supposed cavalryman, and only moments later, his last shout.

Ramon said, "Something's happened to Manuel. We've got to go help him!" He started in the direction of the shout.

Jose caught his arm. "If we go charging out there we can all be in trouble. Let's scout it out first and see what we're facing. I can't stop you, but I'm advising you to stay with the rest of us. If you insist on going out, just take a look around. If they spot you, get back here fast. Don't try to do anything by yourself."

There was no dissuading Ramon. As soon as Jose relaxed his hold he was gone.

"Let's hope for the best and prepare for the worst. It's possible that help is on the way but we sure can't count on it. Get your rifles at the ready just like they're good. Get your bayonets out."

In addition to readying a useless rifle, Victor laid out his slingshot and a well-rounded stone on the ledge beside the rifle.

"You're going to need more than a slingshot to stop those Indians. They aren't like your rabbits."

Victor would have to tell them about David and
Goliath some day.

They waited for a few very long minutes.

From the direction Ramon and Manuel had gone there
arose a commotion of running feet and pounding hooves.
Ramon was running ahead of three mounted Indians.
The horses were gaining fast.

The Indians were loading and discharging their arrows
on the run, one after the other with only moments
between shots. The arrows missed their targets so far.
The lead rider put his bow aside in favor of a tomahawk.

Victor's slingshot whirled while the others raised their
rifles. The rock was released just before the Indian's tomahawk started its downward ark toward Ramon's skull.

Only the horse knew where the rock struck . . . and it
was effective.

The horse jumped, throwing its rider over its neck and
head square into Ramon's back. Both the Indian and
Ramon came tumbling into the depression together. All
nine were on the fallen Indian before he could recover.
Jose saw that the immediate situation was under control
so he turned his attention back to the other Indians.

They had pulled back to be joined by six more warriors. They surveyed the scene. What kind of weapon
brought down their comrade's horse?

During the pause, Jose and Hector brought out their
slingshots and all three gathered a supply of stones.

Ramon said, "They got Manuel. He looked like a pin-
cushion with all those arrows sticking out of him. He
died with his blade in his hand. Didn't look like he had a
chance to use it, though. I thought I might try to get by
them and find help but they were between me and where
I was going. I tried to go around them but they saw me
and I ran. They must have shot a couple dozen arrows at
me. I kept seeing them go right by me. I thought the next
one would get me for sure. I guess it's hard to hit a moving target from the back of a running horse, or maybe
I'm lucky or charmed or something!"

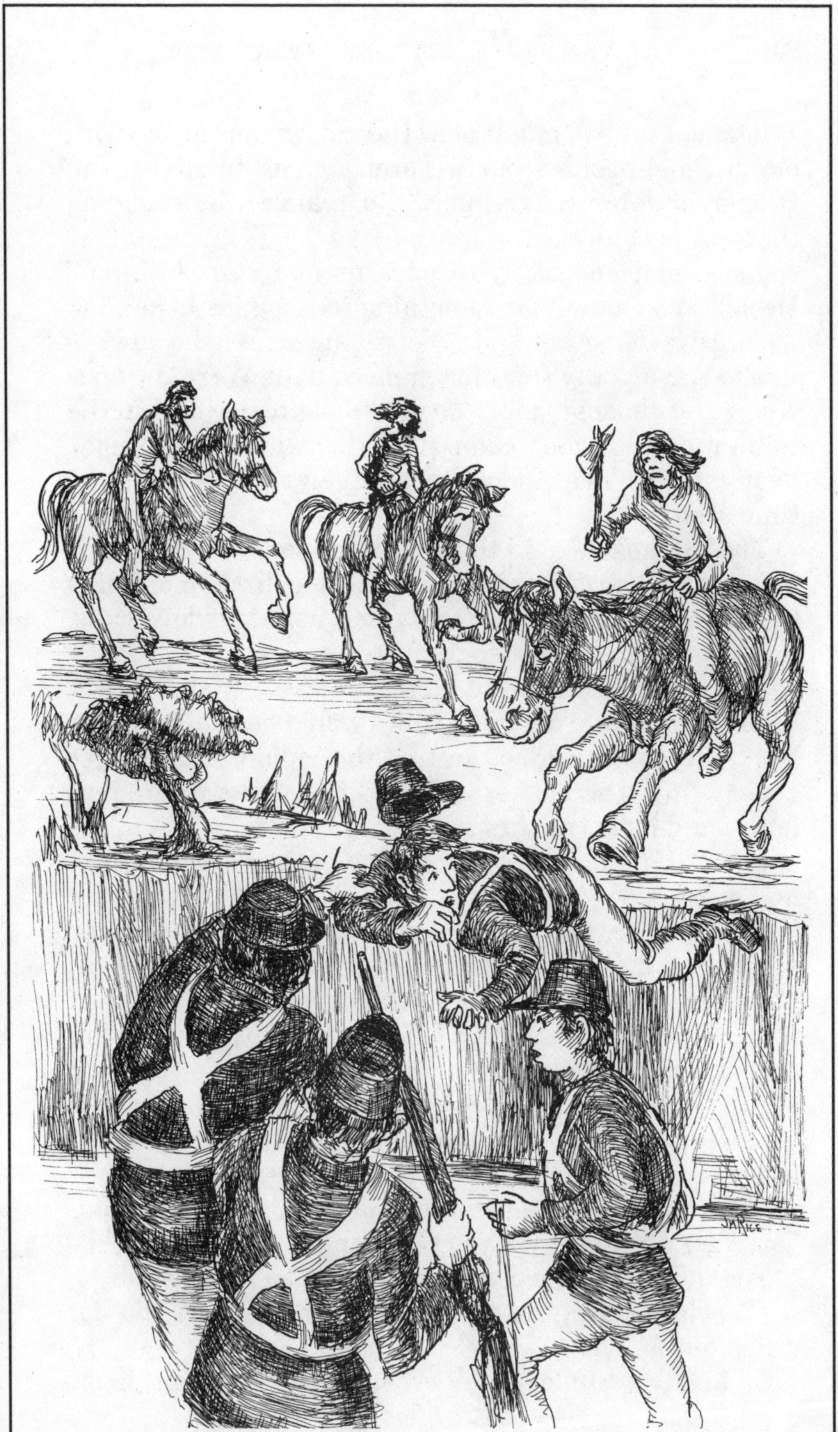

Jose cut in, "We might slow them down for awhile with our little slingshots but we aren't going to stop them. Sooner or later they're going to realize we're holding them off with toys."

"Isn't someone likely to miss us and start looking?" Hector was looking for something to hang his hopes on.

Jose wasn't optimistic. "We're the ones who always like to travel away from the main column. We're the ones who go off chasing game. We don't hold to one spot in the column and we don't camp near the same squads night by night. No, I'm afraid we're not likely to be missed anytime soon."

The Indians mocked them with the sounds of different animals and birds—the yelp of a coyote, first on one side then the answering call from the other side; dove calls, owl calls. If they hoped to cause terror in the squad, they succeeded. Terror, but not panic.

Every once and a while arrows would be shot at them, but there was enough cover that the Indians couldn't get a clear shot. The bushes deflected the shafts where bullets would have cut through.

If the Indians decided to charge on horseback swinging axes and spears, the small detachment wouldn't have a chance. Anytime an Indian exposed himself for more than a few moments, Victor would get off a shot, often striking either the horse or rider. The mystery of the projectiles caused the Indians to postpone making the final fatal charge.

A long period of silence ensued. No animal calls and no sightings for some minutes. "If they're trying to unnerve us they're succeeding," Ramon said.

Jose answered, "Stay in there, don't relax for a second. You'll get all the action you can handle soon enough."

The quiet continued while the minutes dragged on.

"They're waiting for us to relax our guard. If you do, watch out!"

Suddenly a thunder of hooves charged down on them.

They arose at once with bayoneted rifles to meet the challenge, and probably their doom . . .

"Hold it! Don't shoot!" The cavalry sergeant brought his squad to a halt. Their bright uniforms had never looked so beautiful as they did to Jose's squad at that moment.

Jose answered back, "Don't worry. We can't shoot you, they forgot to give us ammunition. How did you find us?"

"Somebody heard some yelling and we found this guy full of arrows. We asked and looked around to see who was missing and here we are. The Indians took off as soon as they saw a show of force."

Hector bragged, "One of them didn't get away. He won't be bothering us anymore."

"So, which one didn't get away? I don't see anyone."

Hector turned to point toward the fallen Indian. He was gone. "That must have been one tough Indian. We all beat him with our rifle butts and I think a couple of bayonet punctures. I don't know how he walked away from all that."

"I wouldn't worry, he's just human. He probably crawled off somewhere to die. Meanwhile, you'd better saddle up and join the march. You're falling behind even while we talk."

Jose said, "We've got a front half of beef here we'll trade for a ride up to the head of the column." The cool weather preserved the meat well.

"You've got a deal. We'll get one of the wagon masters to cook it up for us. That should be just enough to last us until we reach San Antonio."

"Are we getting close? Is that where all the Texians are?" Victor asked.

The cavalryman laughed, "*Si*, we are getting close, maybe two or three days. Not all the Texians are there. Nobody knows exactly how many. It is said most of them are holed up in an old church at the edge of town so there can't be too many."

After the harrowing experience with the Indians, the boys were only too happy to be near the main body of marchers.

Jose knew some troops from General Cos' division who had been in San Antonio before, having been chased out by Ben Milam's Texians. Since these men were familiar with the city, Jose bombarded his new acquaintances with questions. He shared this information—some truths and many rumors—with his friends:

> San Antonio was the largest, most important city in Texas. The Texians had no real army, just a loosely organized mob. They would probably take off running at the first sight of a real army, though many of Cos' veterans would dispute this.
>
> The Texians were planning a big celebration on February 22, the birthday of one of their big heroes—a man named Washington.
>
> There were many beautiful women waiting for the Mexican army to come and liberate them.
>
> Anything could be had for a price—good-looking women, fine liquor, and a general good time.
>
> The army would be paid and given a night on the city before getting down to the business of expelling the Texians.

Any army camp is a fertile ground for the cultivation of rumors. At a time of impending action or during any transition, rumors are particularly rampant. Jose's squad had never been officially assigned to a specific unit, and since they had been traveling near General Cos' regiment (and since his unit was under strength), Jose's little squad was absorbed into Cos' organization.

Vincenti Ramirez also knew about San Antonio. He had been there before, holed up in that same building where the Texians were now, the former church building now called "Alamo." A small group of Texians led by Ben Milam had starved them out and paroled them back to Mexico with the promise they would not raise arms against the Texians again. Generalissimo Santa Anna had forced them to break that parole and now they were back, with the positions reversed.

"That old church is indefensible. We had them outnumbered six or eight to one, and they sent us running. Now we have ten to one in our favor and we have them cornered in that same church. We won't be here long." Vincenti was entertaining a willing audience.

Jose asked, "Do you think we'll get permission to go to the town before we face off the Texians?"

Vincenti laughed. "I don't know about the 'permission.' I was in the city last night; I know how to slip in and out. Most of the civilians in San Antonio are Mexican, like us, so it is easy to put on civilian clothes and mix with them. In fact, I'm going back tonight. They're having a big fandango. There'll be lots of women, dancing, drinking, and fun!"

"Can we go? I haven't had any real fun since I don't know when."

"Well, I don't know . . . maybe. Do you have any civilian clothes? It will help if you have money. Do you?"

Jose was interested. "We can take off our tunics and *tapas* and we're all civilians. We'll be paid something before we get to San Antonio, won't we?"

"The clothes shouldn't be a problem for most of you, but I don't think we can count on being paid anytime soon." Vincenti was not encouraging.

———

Victor had a secret. Something he had not told anyone since his conscription. Shortly after joining the march he had discovered the mysterious coin in his pocket, the coin placed there by his mother. How or why the coin found its way into his pocket he had no idea, and he was not one to question good fortune. Thus far on the march they had not had any need for money, but there was the possibility that Victor would need some for his return home.

Should he share the coin with his friends and hope they would pay him back, or should he hold onto it for future security? In his mind, fate had placed the coin in his possession; fate would provide for the future. Here was the opportunity to explore the pleasures Vincenti said could be found in the big city, along with the guides to show him just where in the city those pleasures could be found.

Victor made his decision: "I have some money—a coin I found in my pocket after I left home. Maybe we could divide it and you could pay me back later."

Jose laughed. "That's good of you, Victor, you are a real buddy, but I am afraid we'll need more than a single peso for a good time for all of us."

Victor had no idea of the value of most money but he had seen a few pesos before. "I don't think my coin is a peso. It is smaller and of a different color."

"Let me see this coin you speak of."

Victor reached in his pocket, pulled out his hand, and opened it to reveal a shiny gold coin. The others looked on, wide-eyed.

Vincenti said, "Dust off your best clothes, boys. Tonight we're going to have a real good time."

—◈—

The day was free. The first free day since Laredo. It was not a pretty day—not as bad as the previous days of the norther—but it was wet and cold with mud everywhere. They had pitched makeshift tents but they weren't very effective. The troops had their orders for the rest period. They were told to rest and prepare for the impending action that would take place over the next few days. Under no circumstances was anyone to go into the city.

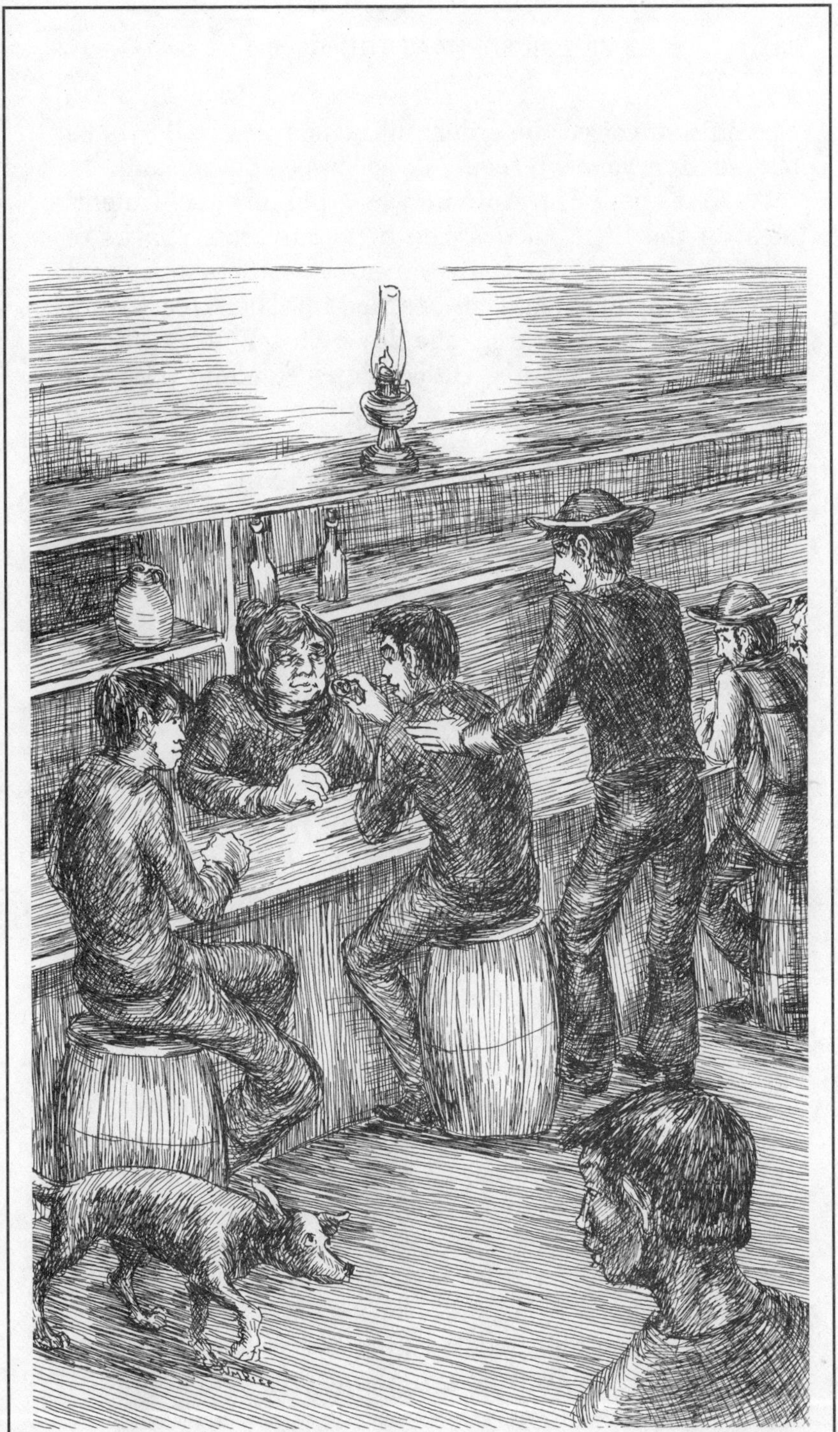

The officers voiced the order, but no one expected it to be obeyed. Everyone who could do so slipped out of camp.

At first sight, San Antonio was a big disappointment. Most of the little *jacales,* the little one-room shacks of mud with straw roofs, were empty. Stores appeared closed; many of them were boarded up. The streets were muddy and slippery from the day's rain. Vincenti didn't seem disturbed by this. He continued leading them up one street, down another, through an alley to where more buildings showed lights. He led them into one.

A fat, middle-aged woman tended a dimly lit bar. Two nondescript men sat at the far end, nursing glasses of warm beer. A single oil lamp barely punctured the darkness. All the occupants were Mexican.

Vincenti addressed the barmaid. "Señora, we need a bottle of good whiskey."

"Since when did a *péon* such as yourself have the price of a drink, much less a bottle?"

"We have the money. Do you have the change for a real piece of gold? Show her your coin, Victor."

Victor slowly took the coin from his pocket and handed it to the señora. She produced a bottle of amber liquid and counted out a handful of change on the bar. Vincenti divided it into equal stacks. One each in front of himself, Victor, Jose, and Hector. Victor was not consulted about the distribution of his money.

The señora spoke again. "I suppose you boys are getting ready to go to the big fandango tonight?"

Vincenti answered, "I heard of a celebration tonight, but the city looks dead to me. What is this celebration and where is it happening?"

"It's George Washington's birthday, some big hero to all these Texians. Just keep going down this street about a quarter mile and you'll come to this big building that's all lit up. There'll be plenty of good fiddling and foot stomping. That big Texian called 'Kwocky' will be fiddling. All those boys from the Alamo will be there. Most of the townspeople are finding excuses to get out of town what with all the stories about Santa Anna's army marching up from Mexico. Some say he's just a few miles out of town right now. I'll bet you boys know something about that."

Jose was suddenly nervous. "It's about time for us to get on down the road if we're going to catch that fandango."

The señora laughed, "Don't worry, honey, I'm neutral. I'm for whoever has the price of a drink. Mexican or Texian, makes no difference to me. I spotted you when you walked in the door. You boy," she pointed toward Vincenti, "you I remember from before, when General Cos was here. Does the Generalissimo know you boys slipped away to come to town? Ha—I won't tell him! Your enemies, the Texians, aren't going to notice a few more Mexican boys at their party. By the time you get there they're going to be too drinked up to tell the difference if you decided to show up in full uniform. I don't think any of them have uniforms to begin with, anybody but that smart aleck Colonel Travis. No, don't worry boys, nobody's going to bother you."

Jose was impatient. "Let's go boys, that party's going to be over before we get there if we don't hurry!"

Outside Vincenti tipped the bottle and took a long swallow. After catching his breath he said, "Oh, is that good stuff," and handed it to Jose, who took his swallow and passed it to Hector. Each in turn commented about the high quality of the hard liquor. Victor was last. The strongest drink he had ever had was homemade blackberry wine El Viejo had made. He took a generous swallow like he had seen the others do. The fiery liquid took his breath away for several seconds.

"What's the matter? Too strong for you? Here, it's my turn again," Vincenti reached for the bottle.

"Oh no, it's not too strong for me. I was just holding it in my mouth to enjoy it longer."

The others laughed at Victor's obvious lie.

Jose offered some advice: "Amigo, it is all right to take the big mouthful, but swallow it slowly, bit by bit, or you'll choke yourself. You'll get sick if you drink it too fast."

The bottle made the rounds at least three more times before they reached their destination.

Vincenti hid the bottle in some bushes beside an adjoining building to the dance hall.

"I think it's better if we leave this outside. Whenever anyone wants a drink he can come out here. Try not to be too obvious—we don't want someone coming along and stealing it."

The dance hall was a large, low-ceilinged room dimly illuminated by lamps suspended from exposed beams. The floor was hard-packed dirt, the walls mostly adobe with some wooden sections. The furniture was made of rough-hewn logs and packing boxes constructed by unskilled laborers. Boards thrown across wooden barrels served as the bar.

Victor felt strangely lightheaded as he lingered behind the others going into the long, rambling room. One wouldn't suspect that a large part of the population had left town; the place was crowded. Many of the guests were tall, light-skinned men who spoke a strange language that Victor could not understand. Music came from a small raised platform at the opposite end of the building. The main musician, the one he took to be the one the bartender had spoken of, the one she called Kwocky, played the fiddle. He was taller than most Mexicans Victor knew. He wore a strange animal skin cap. He laughed and joked between numbers. Whatever he said, it must have been very entertaining, judging by the reaction of his audience. For just a second, the fiddler's eyes met Victor's. In that instant the humor was gone. Kwocky raised his finger to point toward Victor and sighted along it as though it were a weapon and those eyes bore through him to reveal all his secrets, then they shifted back to the frivolity of the occasion as though nothing unusual had happened. It had been so fast and smooth that no one else seemed to have noticed. Was it just a passing gesture? Had he imagined it? No.

Victor was fascinated by the Texians. He tried to detect the quality that would prompt the entire Mexican army to march nearly four hundred miles to chase them back north. They were mostly young; Kwocky at nearly fifty years of age was most likely the oldest. The young Texians laughed, danced, and flirted with the girls. What was the threat? Victor wondered.

He tried to pick out the military leaders.

One was apparent: a young man in his twenties, slight of build, with sandy hair. He was the only person in full dress uniform—too fancy for an enlisted man. He stood erect, apart from the revelers, nursing a drink. Something weighed heavily on his mind. Could this young man be the commander, the one called Travis?

A third man among the Texians stood out. Tall, dark, and heavily built, he had none of the vestments of the younger officer Travis. The only military item on his person was a wicked-looking knife hanging in a sheath from his belt. He put on a show of laughing and joking with his comrades but his celebrating was strained, as though he didn't feel well. He looked very rugged, not the kind one would want to meet in a fight, even in his seemingly weakened state. This man seemed equally at ease speaking Spanish. Victor could close his eyes and not identify a trace of foreign accent in his speech. This would be the famous knife-fighter, James ("Jim") Bowie.

Another group stood out despite its efforts to appear inconspicuous. They were Hispanic, but they were markedly different from the other Mexicans present. They were lighter skinned and better dressed. The apparent leader of the group was also tall—the only others of similar height were the Texians, Kwocky, and Bowie. This man seemed to be studying the room and its occupants with more than a casual interest. He had a glass in his

hand but he did not drink. His eyes held the most intense
gaze Victor had seen in any man. He made it a point to
avert his eyes when those penetrating glances shifted in
his direction. He was afraid he would react in an obvious
way to their intensity. The eyes seemed to hold a special
power over all they beheld. This man and his small group
stayed in the shadow at the edge of the party crowd.
Others in the room were too preoccupied with drinking
and dancing to take notice of the wallflowers.

Victor continued his observations but no one else
caught his eye. Most in the room appeared to be only
intent on having a good time. These Texians certainly
didn't seem very dangerous. Over half of the garrison
from the Alamo were in that room. They didn't appear
frightened or intimidated. Did they have any idea of the
force that was threatening them?

Sergeant Pena was right. As soon as those Texians
realized what they were up against, as soon as Santa
Anna made his show of force, they would see the hope-
lessness of their situation and run.

A hand clasped down on his shoulder. *"Holà,* Victor,
what are you doing over here all by yourself?" It was
Jose. "Come on over where there is fun to be had.
Vincenti wants to introduce us to some girls. You are getting behind, here," and he placed a full glass in Victor's
hand. "Come on, drink up." The bottle had not remained
outside for long.

He led Victor to a small, makeshift table near the end
of the bar where Vincenti, Hector, and four señoritas
awaited them. Vincenti stood up, "Victor—Amigo!" He was
a few drinks ahead of Victor and the whiskey had loosened his tongue considerably. "Victor, I want you to meet
Rosa. She has been admiring you from across the room."

Both Victor and Rosa turned several shades of red at
Vincenti's exaggerated introduction. Rosa was the oldest
of the four señoritas, and more than a few years older
than Victor. She was pretty in a worn sort of way; she had

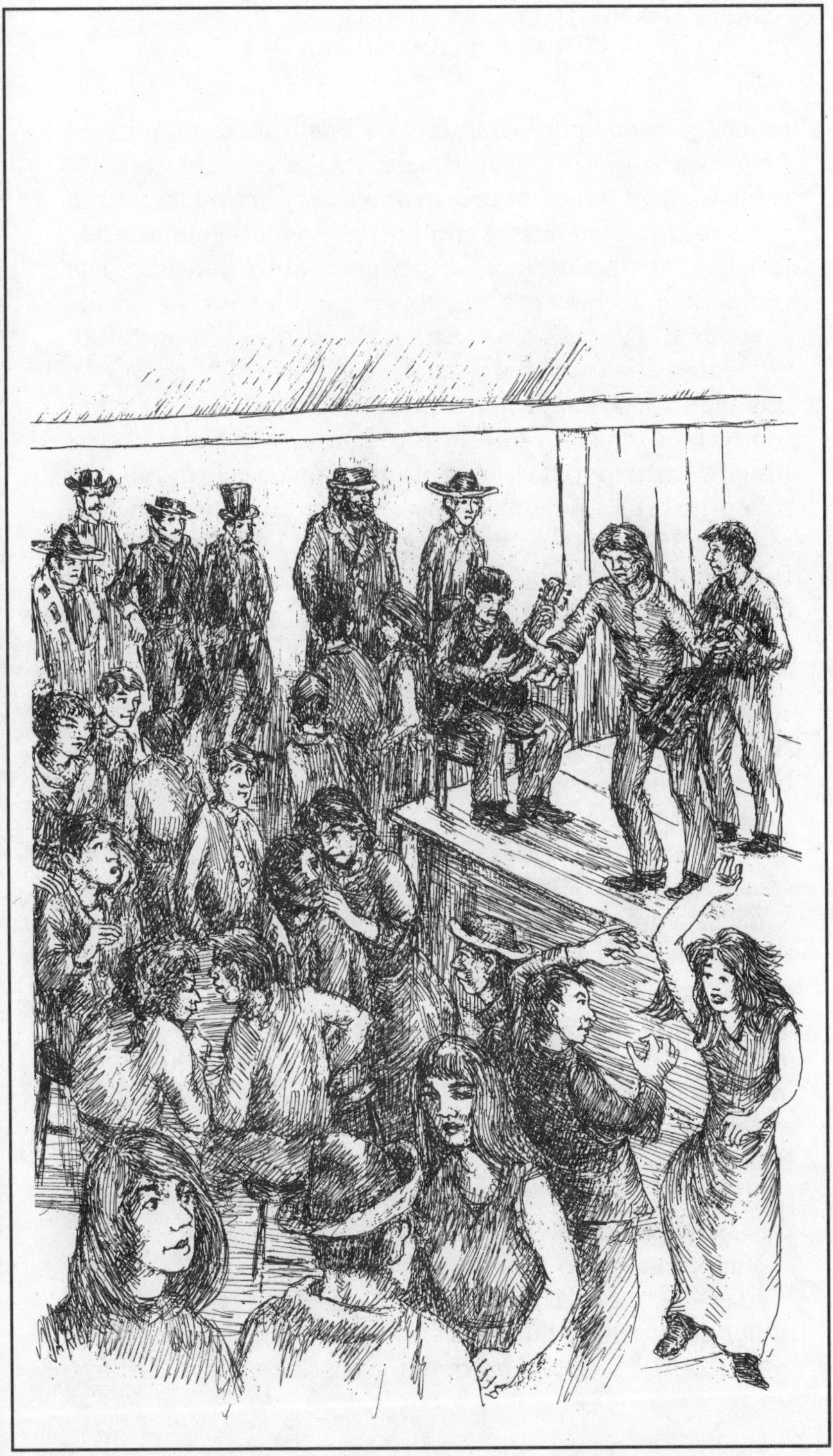

probably been more attractive when she was younger. After two more drinks all the girls were younger and better looking; three more drinks and they were all beautiful!

Rosa squeezed Victor's hand under the table and led him out to the area where people were dancing. The rousing music, Rosa's perfume, and the whiskey succeeded in clouding Victor's mind and completely enveloped his senses. He had never been this close to a girl before. He could not understand what was happening to him, but he liked it. She leaned close and kissed him and whispered something in his ear. He couldn't be sure what she said, but it sounded like an invitation. She grasped his arm firmly and guided him away from the table, out the door and into a small room in a building down the street from the fandango.

———

A bright beam of light pierced his stupor many hours later. The beam exploded in the back of his head when he tried to rise.

"How are you this morning, lover boy?" Rosa approached him with a cup of steaming coffee.

Victor didn't know how to answer. The previous evening was a complete blank to him. He took the coffee in both shaking hands and replied a simple "gracias."

She could see his discomfort but she wouldn't let him off the hook immediately. "You aren't really a heavy drinker, are you?"

"A little wine now and then, but this is the first time I've had real whiskey."

"Oh, I would never have guessed. I suppose you are a real lady's man too, huh?"

Victor stammered in embarrassment, "W-well . . . "

Rosa laughed. "Don't worry. Your virtue is intact. You didn't do anything but pass out. You're probably just tired after the long march and the unaccustomed drinks didn't

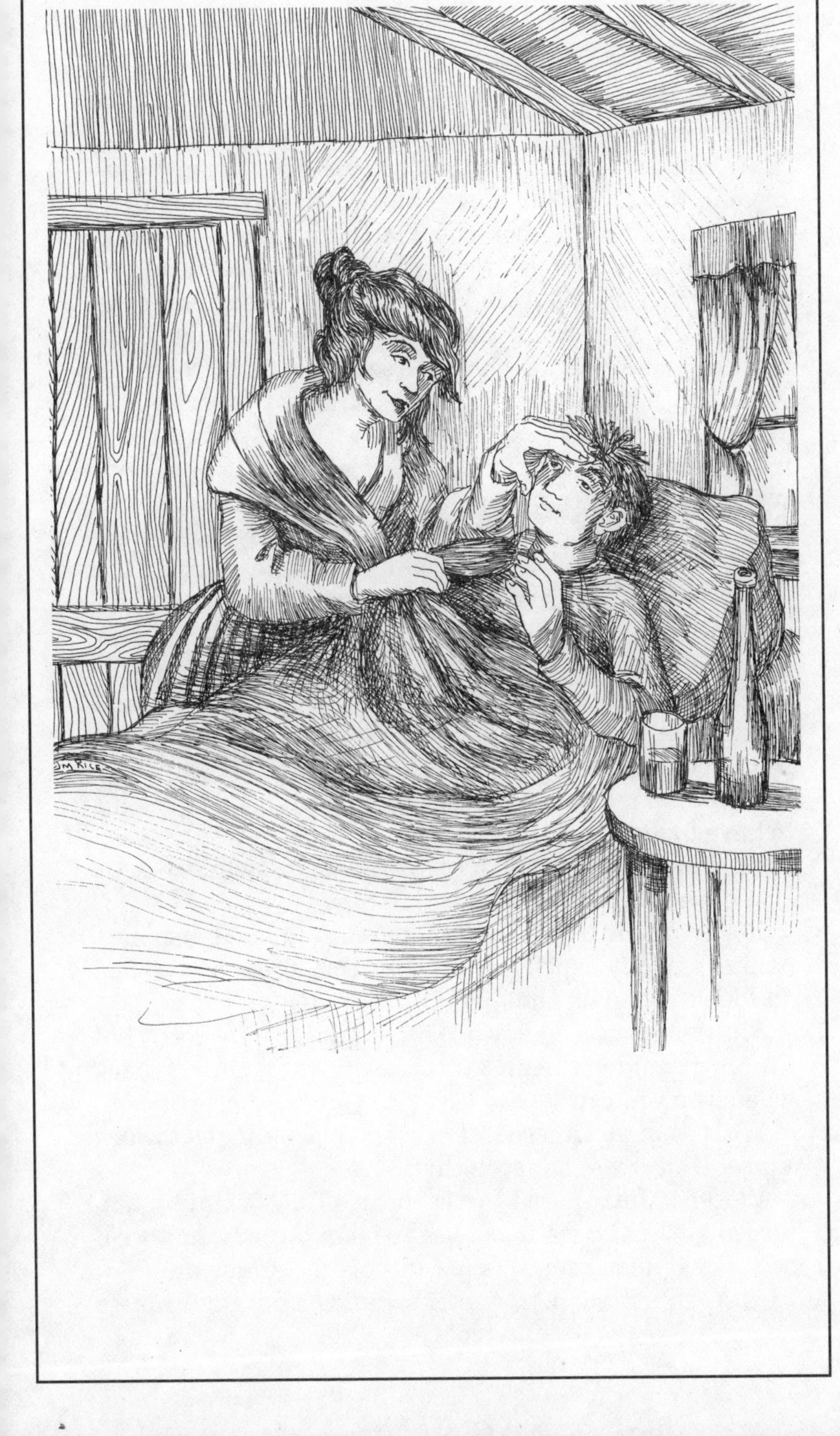
JM RICE

help. Finish your coffee and I'll cook you some breakfast. You'll feel better with a hot meal under your belt."

He did feel much better after his first home-cooked meal in weeks. The meal was hardly finished when there was a knock on the door. His heart did a double flip. Had the army sent someone out for him, for desertion? He had heard of Santa Anna's penalties for desertion, ranging all the way from extra duty to flogging or to the extreme case he had heard: a soldier had to serve ten extra years in the army without pay. Or worse: had the Texians come for him? He was sure Kwocky had recognized him for a Mexican soldier last night. The small room offered no hiding places and no exits besides the entrance door where someone was knocking. The single window was too small and too high to serve as an exit. It was too late to do anything but face whatever was on the other side of the door. Rosa opened the door. "Holà, Vincenti, *como esta*? How are you doing this morning?"

"Buena, gracias. I came back for my amigo, Victor. I took the others back last night. None of us got past the front door with our women. I didn't have the heart to disturb your romantic evening. *Venga,* Victor, we are going to have to hurry and watch our step in the daylight to get back. Jose and Hector can cover for us for awhile, but we still have to hurry!"

Rosa came to Victor. Before he realized what was happening she enveloped him in her arms, drew him to her, and kissed him on the lips.

She whispered softly to him, but not so soft that Vincenti could not hear: "Adios, my lover boy. Come back whenever you can."

What had he missed? He looked pleadingly toward Vincenti. "Do you suppose that . . . "

Vincenti anticipated the request. "No! Absolutely not. Last night will have to do. We are late already, and we'll be lucky if our absence is not discovered. Come on!"

Rosa squeezed both Victor's hands and gave him a

peck on the cheek as she guided him out the door.

She gave him one more smile. "Adios, lover!" She closed the door behind him.

———◦-◦-◦———

Victor's hangover was brief. The quantity of alcohol he had consumed was not great. His inexperience combined with the heady atmosphere had served to increase his susceptibility to intoxication. The cool winter breeze brought his senses into focus almost at once.

"It is no joke. We must hurry. The Generalissimo is having all the troops fall in for a full dress parade for the Texians. You must tell us all about last night—we are all dying to hear. You are the only one of the four to get lucky, you know. Some of the guests were making us nervous and we thought it best to get out of sight."

They walked at a leisurely pace to the edge of town, then sped up. Vincenti advised, "Nothing attracts attention like two people running. In this situation it could get a person shot or at least stopped for questioning, from either side. I don't think we could stand up to questioning from anybody.

As soon as they were out of sight, Vincenti broke into a ground-covering Indian trot, a pace he appeared capable of holding all day. Victor could barely keep up.

They found the main body of soldiers split into small groups practicing marching in step and carrying their weapons properly. Jose was having some complications, especially with the Indians, who did not speak the language. Victor caught on pretty fast after Jose gave him a small pebble to hold in his left hand. Vincenti already knew about the marching in step. After an hour of somewhat productive practice, Jose called them to a halt for a rest period. "Hey, Victor, you did all right for yourself last night, eh? I'm glad somebody did. When are you going to tell us about it?"

Victor looked down and made a sheepish grin, which the others took for shyness. He would have some trouble giving them details about something that didn't happen. Let them continue to believe shyness prevented his discussing the "affair."

"You didn't miss much this morning, just instructions on how to load and fire your weapon and of course everyone already knows that."

Victor wanted to speak up, no one had given him that kind of information, but he didn't want to appear stupid. If they found out the truth about last night besides the fact that he didn't know how to use a weapon, he was sure he would be teased. It would be open season on Victor Lopez.

"Let's get back to the marching practice. The sergeant will be here soon to show us how to use our weapons in a combat situation."

At the end of another hour they weren't much better, but Jose and Vincenti thought they might do well enough so long as they marched straight ahead without turning or trying to start and stop.

The sergeant soon appeared—a short man in his early forties, decked out in full uniform. He gathered four squads in a single group for his instructional session.

"*Attençion!*" His shout threw the entire collection into a state of confusion. Everyone looked toward the veterans to see what to do. The sergeant shook his head in dismay. "I see we have a ways to go. We'll dispense with close-order drill for the moment and go straight to the important stuff. All of you will be out in full uniform in the morning as we march into the position of siege. The Generalissimo himself will inspect the troops before we move forward. We hope our mere appearance will put such fear into the Texians that they will surrender without a fight, but in the event that they do not surrender I will show you how a soldier makes a charge. There will be hundreds of us moving forward at once, putting out a solid wall of fire, so it will not be necessary to aim. You will carry your weapon like this, at a forty-five degree angle to the ground with the muzzle pointed toward the top of the fortress wall. The firepower will be so dense that anything showing above the wall will be shot to pieces.

He had the entire company hold their weapons alongside their bodies at the required forty-five degree angle. They all rushed forward clicking the hammers. He had them do their mock charges several times until he was sure everyone had it correct. He showed them how to attach their bayonets and make several more charges, ripping their imaginary enemies to shreds at the end of each charge. No one could survive such savage attacks as those mounted by the troops in their mock battle.

"*Attençion, soldados, oje!* I'll leave you to get ready for tomorrow. Dust off your uniforms, practice what I've shown you, and keep in mind the Generalissimo himself will inspect you tomorrow. Before I leave I have two promotions to hand down. Vincenti Rodriquiz: you are promoted to corporal with corresponding pay raise from seven pesos per week to ten pesos per week. Jose Gomez: you are promoted to sergeant with a pay raise from seven to twelve pesos per week. What are you going to do with all that extra money?"

He came to attention, saluted, and walked stiffly away.

Before Jose and Vincenti decided what to do with the extra pesos, they might try to find out what happened to the first *seven* pesos. So far none of the squad had received a single centavo on the march.

Jose and Vincenti instructed the squad to practice their drill and get their uniforms in shape while they withdrew to sew their new stripes on their sleeves. The squad fumbled through a few drills, dusted off their jackets, and went to bed. Victor tried to concentrate on the challenges of the approaching day, but his mind kept slipping back to the previous night and what might have happened if he hadn't acted so foolishly.

The troops were awakened by the sound of bugles. All up and down the line, the various units had kept in close proximity so they could form up easier on the big day. Amid much shouting and confusion some semblance of order was reached. All the troops faced the same direction and all rifles were shouldered with muzzles pointing in an upward direction.

The cavalry formed up in a much more orderly fashion. They all consisted of more experienced troops of officer and non-commissioned officer rank.

The entire army in formation made for a formidable sight.

Far down the line, a small group of mounted officers started a slow ceremonial parade before the long columns. Excited whispers sounded in the ranks: "Here he comes. . . Is it really him? It is! It's the Generalissimo and his staff . . . "

As he approached, the voices of the troops were hushed. His uniform reflected light from many medals. Silver and gold decorated his buttons, buckles, and saddle trimmings. His hat was trimmed in white animal fur. His staff was dressed only slightly less extravagantly. There was something familiar about that group. Victor couldn't distinguish details of the faces, but as they came nearer, he was aware of something very disturbing about the whole entourage of the famous Generalissimo. Then he was in front of Victor and their eyes met for a terrible instant and the recognition struck him. Those eyes that drilled through the soul . . . those unsmiling eyes so powerful in their gaze . . . those same eyes he remembered from the fandango! He feared for a moment that this powerful man would suddenly unsheathe his fancy sword and cut him down on the spot. After the brief meeting of the eyes, Generalissimo Santa Anna gave no further sign of recognition. The pause had been so slight that no one else could have noticed. Victor had a deep-down fear that he had been singled out for some terrible fate. He was happy when the high brass moved on down the line. An eternity later, drums rolled and bugles sounded all up and down the line, and the whole army—foot soldiers, cavalry, and wagons—moved out together.

Victor felt himself swelling with pride to be a part of such an impressive organization. There must be a very noble cause to drive such an array of military display. Jose and Vincenti appeared to have added inches to their height as they marched tall at the head of the little squad. The rifle rested easily on his shoulder; its cumbersome weight seemed to have lightened. They paraded in long columns in front of the little garrison called "The Alamo" so all those inside could see what they faced. The cavalry galloped alongside the infantry between it and the Alamo. Here were thousands of troops in full uniform facing a force that boasted of only one uniform, and that one furnished by its wearer.

The infantry took their posts several yards behind a row of *jacales* that offered only partial concealment from the eyes of the Texians.

Well to the rear but within sight of the proceedings was Santa Anna with his entourage. A senior cavalry officer with flashing medals and weapons conferred with the Generalissimo. He wheeled his horse around and rode toward the Texian stronghold carrying a white banner aloft.

"*Qué pasa?* What is going on?" The procedures were a mystery to Victor.

Vincenti, who had been at the Alamo before when the roles were reversed, answered, "Santa Anna is sending out his representative under a flag of truce. He is delivering the terms of surrender to the Texians. They will lay down their weapons, promise never to bear arms against the Republic of Mexico again, and Santa Anna will parole them back to where they came from up north somewhere in the United States, I think."

Jose added, "Just think Victor, it will all be finished this evening and you can spend the night back in the

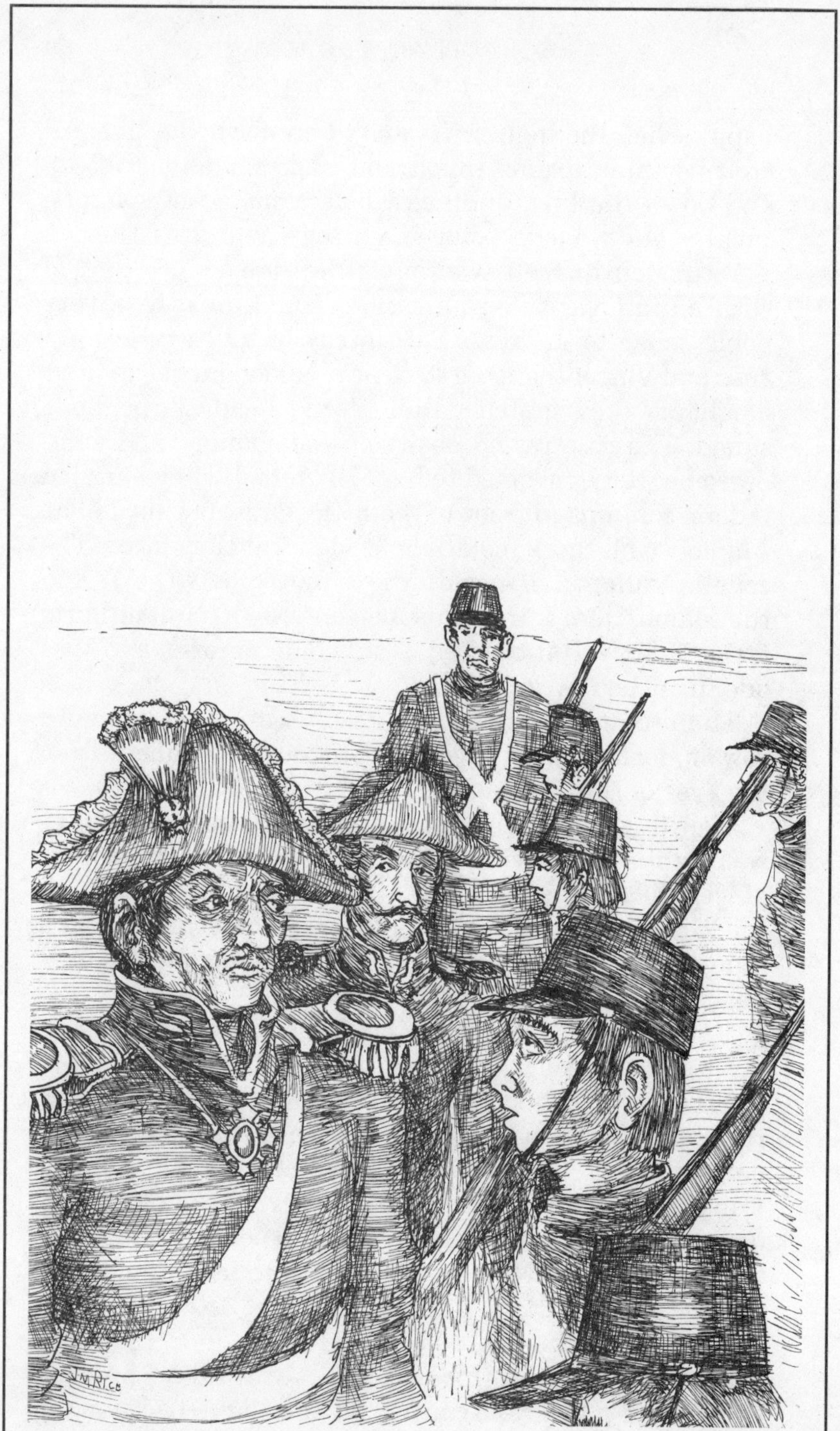
J.M. Rice

arms of your sweet Rosa. They will probably pay us before we go marching off across Texas to accept the surrender of the rest of the rebels. That will be nice, to have another night on the town. Maybe the rest of us can finish what we started."

Hector added, "Victor got a head start. It's time the rest of us got a chance to catch up."

The Mexican peace emissary approached the gate to the Texians' fortress. It opened and he entered. Only moments later he came charging out, riding as hard as his mount could go. Seconds later there was the roar of the Texians' giant eighteen-pound cannon. Somewhere out behind them, an empty building was transformed to dust and splinters.

Victor glanced around at the others. "I guess this means I won't be visiting Rosa tonight, huh?"

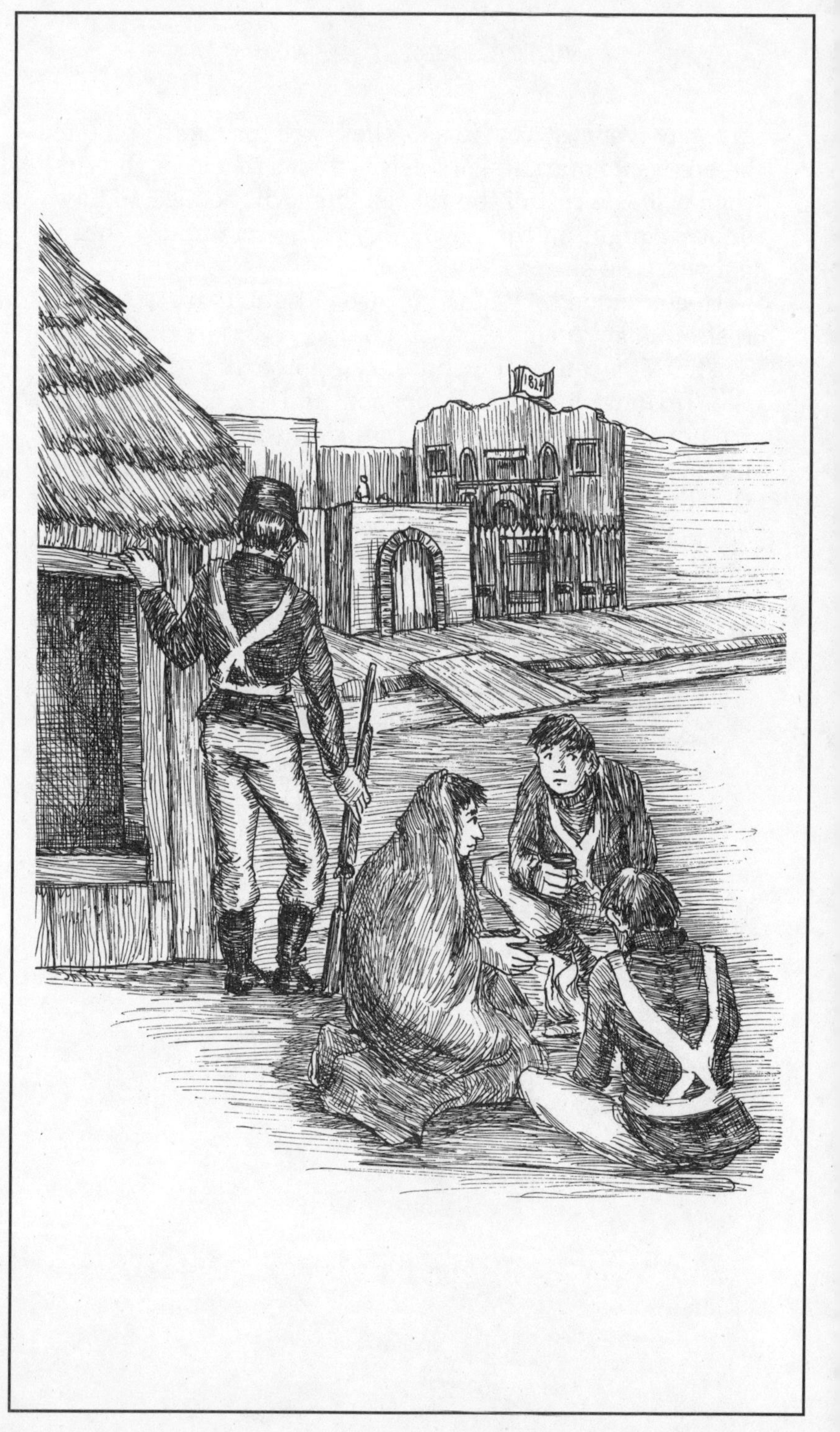
1824

6

THEY LAUGHED.

Jose said, "Not tonight I'm afraid. We're going to have to chase them out. It'll be tomorrow or the day after at least before we finish this job."

The Mexican artillery answered with its own barrage. Most of the cannon balls fell short while others bounced harmlessly off the walls of the Alamo. Rifle fire fell far short. The Mexican rifles had a very limited range.

On the south wall of the Alamo, a tall Texian wearing an unusual animal skin cap, the one called "Kwocky," carefully loaded his long hunting rifle. It was a special rifle given to him by various admirers back in Tennessee for political accomplishments. Kwocky, or Crockett, as it was spelled back up north, placed great value on his prized rifle, such that he even gave it a name, Betsy. He put an extra charge of powder and picked a perfectly formed ball. He rammed charge and ball firmly down the long balanced barrel. He took a lying-down position on the wall and sighted down the barrel, searching for one target among many out beyond the *jacales*. There were many Mexicans out there, standing or milling about, visible between the shacks. The range was far, perhaps too far, even for his special Betsy.

Jose's little squad stood transfixed by the sudden turn of events. What was to have been a short demonstration to intimidate a handful of rebels in an impossible position had escalated to something no one understood. It was a tense situation.

The tension grew too much for Jose: he wanted action—any kind of action. He jumped to the top of a nearby mound of dirt, held his gun at arms' length, and shouted toward the Texians: *"Viva Mejico! Viva Mej . . . "*

A small puff of smoke arose from the south wall of the Alamo and Jose didn't complete his sentence. At first the others thought Jose had slipped on the slick muddy earth, wet by the recent rain. The bullet struck before the sound of it firing reached their ears. Victor ran to Jose to help him to his feet. "Jose, let me help you! Jose! What's the matter? Come on, you've got to help Hector and me run that cattle ranch!" Victor tried to shake Jose awake and only then did he see the blood seeping through the tunic. Jose had the distinction of being the first soldier to fall in the battle of the Alamo.

Jose was dead. Victor and Hector would have to run the ranch without Jose. It was hard for Victor to grasp this fact. One moment his friend was alive and shouting at the Texians, and the next he was lying there limp and lifeless with a growing red splotch across his chest. Few of the Mexican troops saw the small puff of smoke or heard the report of David Crockett's long rifle that ended the short life of Sergeant Jose Gomez. The few answering shots from the Mexican lines fell far short. There were no answering shots from Jose's squad. They had not been issued ammunition yet.

———◦—◦———

Victor was overcome with grief. He had never witnessed the death of anyone close to him. He insisted on digging the grave himself. He could find nothing on the body to suggest next of kin. A faded letter written in a feminine hand suggested a past romance, but she had grown tired of waiting. She was going to wed another. There was no return address.

Victor wrapped the body in his precious blanket from home and together they lowered it into the shallow grave.

The water at the bottom turned into a slurry mixture as the newly removed mud was pushed back into the hole.

It was suddenly damp and chilly. The excitement, the feeling of elation, the pride of being part of something grand, had melted. It had all become part of the cold gray dampness of the day. Those who remained of Jose's little squad went into the nearest empty *jacale*. They were all empty now.

Ramon pulled some straw from the inside of the roof, and with some sticks removed from the walls and pieces of broken furniture, they started a small fire. Outside, the bugles wailed the plaintiff tones of the *doguello*, the signal for "no quarter," and from the roof of San Fernando Cathedral the blood red flag reinforcing the bugle call was raised. The boys huddled close to the small fire. The drama of the moment was lost on them.

Hector spoke to Victor, "What are we going to do about our plans for the ranch? Do we just forget about it?"

"No, we've got to have something to hang on to. The two of us can still do it. I think we need to bring the memory of Jose into it, though. I know how we can do it: real vaqueros burn their marks on their cattle. We can make our mark for the three of us, a mixture of *J, H,* and *V* or something, showing all three, with part of one letter also being part of another.

"Let's put curve marks on the outside letters so they look like wings to show that Jose has passed on."

Both young men went to sleep with a dream that night.

———◦———

They awoke to the sounds of bugles blowing a wake-up call as much for the benefit of the Texians as for the Mexicans. The soldiers formed up and put on a marching show for the Texians. They were rewarded with a volley of rifle fire. One more Mexican soldier fell dead and three suffered minor wounds. The show ended and the marchers withdrew to a less conspicuous position.

Mexican artillery answered the rifle fire and once again cannon balls bounced harmlessly off thick walls. No Texians were injured in the barrage.

The squad, now Vincenti's squad, retired to their jacale and tried to stay warm around the little fire. After a while a messenger came around. He delivered six rounds of ammunition for each soldier and said,

"Tomorrow is the day. We're going to get those Texians out once and for all. Be ready to form up when the word comes down."

The next morning was another awakening to bugles and cannons. During the night the cannons had been moved closer to the Texians' fortress. Still the little eight-pound guns only chipped away at the walls. Word was there were larger, twelve-pound cannons being brought up, but they were days away. The troops hurried to be ready whenever the call came, but there was one delay after another. First one group, then the next would brace for the attack. Finally a group of three hundred were chosen to charge the south wall. This wall appeared to be the weakest side of the fort, featuring a gate and a barricade consisting of upright logs. Non-commissioned officers circulated among the troops, giving last-minute instructions and assuring them that one charge should do the job.

The attackers outnumbered the Texians two to one. All they had to do was knock down the log barricade, open the gate, and wipe up. The three hundred men would open the way for the full force to rush in. In preparation for the attack, the cannons opened a continuous artillery barrage to weaken the Texians' defenses. The area became a world of smoke, noise, and confusion. Officers shouted orders that could not be heard. The dark smoke from exploding black powder made visibility close to zero at times. Eyes burned, ears rang, and senses

were jumbled. People became disoriented. It was difficult
to discern where to go and what to do.

Victor was in the middle of a group being pushed and
shoved from one direction to another. The order was given
to charge and suddenly they were nearly all moving in
the same direction. From behind the log barricade
appeared a solid row of Texian rifles. There were more
puffs of black smoke and the solid sound of rifle reports
blending together in one long sound, accented regularly
by the roar of cannons from high atop the wall of the
chapel, on one side and above the gate on the other side.
Every time one of the cannons spoke, large gaps would
appear in the lines as several Mexicans would be cut
down by the deadly grapeshot. Most of the soldiers, Victor
included, were beyond fear. They moved or were pushed
forward. It seemed everybody was going to be cut down.
The front line reached a point about ninety yards from
the wall and one man turned and ran. That was a trigger
to panic that erupted across the front line and quickly
spread throughout the ranks. Victor was knocked down
by the retreating riot. He was knocked down two more
times before he managed to stay on his feet long enough
to join the wild retreat. They reached the lines of *jacales*
and kept running for some distance beyond.

The gate to the Alamo opened and two mounted Texians
emerged, carrying torches. They galloped forward as
though pursuing the retreating Mexicans. A few Mexicans
turned to fire at them, but most were intent on putting as
much space as possible between them and the Texians.
Several troops from the rear, who had not taken part in the
charge, opened fire, but it was as though the torchbearers
were charmed; the Mexican rifles seemed to have no effect.
The only casualty was the eighteen-pound cannon,
knocked off its base. At thirty-five hundred pounds, the
cannon would require some serious manpower to reset it.

The two horsemen rode quickly from one *jacale* to
another, setting each ablaze until all were burning. The
Mexican lines were in such a state of confusion that no

one seemed able to stop the two lone Texians as they completed their acts of arson and returned to the Alamo, unscathed.

Vincenti's squad gathered at what was left of their burned-out *jacale*. It hadn't been much, but it had had a roof and walls for some protection against the weather. Now they were exposed not only to the weather, but also to deadly sniper fire coming from the fortress walls. They soon found it prudent to move back just out of reach of the Texians' long rifles.

———

Meanwhile the Generalissimo was involved in more personal matters. He had met a beautiful young señorita at a social function in San Antonio. The señorita was of very proper upbringing. If Santa Anna expected her to return his romantic advances, he would have to make it "legal" with a marriage ceremony, performed by a priest. But he could not find a priest to legalize the affair. (The fact that he already had a wife back in Mexico tended to complicate his search for an ordained priest willing to bond the two in holy matrimony.) One of Santa Anna's lieutenants who fancied himself an actor volunteered to play the role.

Santa Anna was too preoccupied with his honeymoon to devote his full attention to military matters. It would be a few days before all his troops and supplies caught up with him at San Antonio. He relegated authority to his lieutenants and held the army in siege while he entertained his new bride. The troops on the line couldn't know what was happening in the ranks of senior officers. They were muddy, cold, and generally miserable.

———

The day after the failed charge—February 26—dawned fair and warmer, comfortable only by comparison to the previous days. A short truce ensued, during which the

Mexicans carried or dragged their fallen comrades to the rear for burial or medical attention. The Mexican artillery then resumed a continual harassing fire around the clock. Bugles and drums augmented the noise of the cannons. Neither did much damage to the Texians' stronghold. The infantry had few official duties during this time; some amused themselves by yelling and jeering at the Texians. The Texians returned the insults, but these too were ineffective since few understood the others' language.

Vincenti's squad took advantage of the lull to scrape and wash away some of the mud from the recent rains. They tried to get some rest, but relaxation was difficult with the background noise of bugles blaring and cannons blasting.

Hector and Victor talked about their future as vaqueros and started plans for building their cattle empire. They tried to draw Vincenti into their discussions, but he wanted nothing to do with the cattle business. He would stay with the glamour of life in the military.

The three could agree on one thing—that first night in San Antonio, the night of the fandango.

"I'm tired of listening to you two forevermore talking about your make-believe ranch. Let's talk about something real, something here and now. Let's go into town, look up the señoritas, have a few drinks, and, well, let happen what will," Vincenti said.

Victor wasn't too sure. "We have orders to stay here and watch the Texians. We could get into big trouble."

"What could they do to us that would be worse than what has already happened? Who's going to notice three soldiers slipping away for awhile? We'll be back before morning."

Victor and Hector didn't put up much of an argument. They were bored and as anxious as Vincenti for some excitement. Victor hesitated as he remembered those penetrating eyes of their commander. He could only imagine the wrath of Santa Anna, once aroused. The hesitation was only momentary.

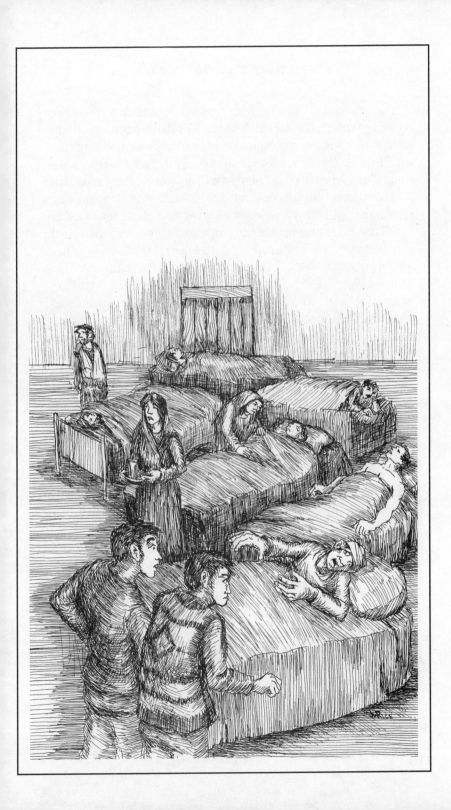

They walked slowly from camp to camp, gradually working their way toward town. The talk around all the campfires was about the day's skirmish and about the conflict to come. Vincenti talked easily with anyone he met. Words didn't come nearly as easy for Victor or Hector. After they broke free of the camps they found few occupied buildings. Some had been hit by Texian artillery, many were boarded up, and some just deserted, the occupants had simply left to escape hostilities. They saw lights at the long building, site of the recent fandango. They heard sounds coming from within, but they were not sounds of celebration. They were sounds of pain, moaning and screaming. Vincenti opened the door and they stepped into a living nightmare. Scattered over the bare floor were dozens of wounded soldiers. Some had blankets, a few had mattresses, a few lay on tables, but most lay on the bare dirt floor. There were torn bodies, missing limbs, and gaping, bleeding wounds. Some were tended by the camp followers. Most lay in their misery, begging for relief. Santa Anna had not seen fit to provide doctors with medical supplies for his army.

Victor hoped that if he were shot it would be like Jose, quick and sure. It would be a fate worse than death to join these pitiable creatures. The three lost no time in getting out of the depressing surroundings.

Vincenti said, "Let's get out of here. We came to town to find a good time, not get involved in a miserable situation like this. Come on, let's find the girls!"

Victor and Hector couldn't build much enthusiasm for the venture, but they needed to break the spell of depression.

"Si, let's find the girls. I've been thinking about Rosa since the other night." Victor said the words but there was no enthusiasm behind them.

Vincenti sensed the diminished ardor. "You can't let something like this get you down. War is like that. You have to live one day at a time. If you start thinking about the bad things that can happen, you'll go crazy. Take

your good times where you find them. The contrast
between the good and bad makes the good times better.
Think about Rosa and the fun you'll have. Tomorrow will
come soon enough."

Victor tried to take Vincenti's advice. He would think
about Rosa, and in his imagination he pictured her
drawing him close, ever closer in a romantic embrace,
only to have this image replaced by one of the broken soldiers he had just seen.

The real live Rosa would erase all those disturbing
images building in his mind. He would hold her in his
arms, pull her close and they would finish what they
started after the fandango. The images of the wounded
soldiers gradually faded as they moved closer to her place.
Anticipation built by the second until he was obsessed
with the thought of their meeting. Had she thought of him
as he had thought of her?

The wounded soldiers were gone from his mind when
they reached her little room. No light showed from her
window or from the cracks around her door. Perhaps she
was asleep early. He knocked and there was no sound
from within.

"She's not there. Look closely. The door's nailed closed.
She's done gone to get away from the conflict. *Lo siento,*
I'm sorry, amigo. This is not your night. We'll go on to the
other girls' places. Maybe they have friends." As far as
Vincenti was concerned, a girl was a girl. One or the
other, what's the difference?

They went to the other girls' places with the same
result.

"I know some other girls in San Antonio, let's not give
up yet."

Vincenti took them to several other houses, but there
would be no female companionship on this night.

They went back to the little bar they had visited
before going to the fandango on their previous visit. It
too was boarded up.

"Es bastante. This is enough. If we can't have a girl we

can at least have a drink." Vincenti found a loose board and pried the door open. Inside, the room still smelled of stale smoke, spilled drinks, and dirt, but the boys didn't notice. Vincenti found two bottles.

Victor was nervous. "Let's get out of here before someone catches us. I didn't figure on going on a stealing spree."

Vincenti had an answer: "We're not stealing. This is part of being a soldier. You take what you need from the enemy. It's called the 'spoils' of war. We're entitled."

Victor didn't understand, but he didn't insist.

Hector said, "It's still not a good idea to hang around and look for trouble."

Vincenti answered, "We'll find more trouble on the street. This isn't a nice place, it's smelly and dark, but it's also warm and dry and there is a place to sit down. Nobody's going to walk into a dingy, dark place that looks closed and deserted."

"We did."

Vincenti ignored him and opened a bottle. He poured drinks into three dirty glasses he found somewhere under the bar. "Remember, boys—sip, don't gulp. We'll be here as long as we like. We're in no hurry. We are the conquering army. We are entitled to take what we want and nobody's going to stop us."

Such talk made Victor uneasy. It sounded very similar to Jose's talk earlier during the blanket incident. Still, what could he do? These were his friends, the only people he could relate to. He knew Vincenti. He wasn't really like that. His words were largely bravado, showing off before his friends.

Hector proposed a toast, "Let's not waste time thinking about what's past. We can't change that and let's not worry about tomorrow. What's going to happen will happen. That leaves today—now. Let's drink to the present. No past. No future. Just now."

That seemed to be something they could agree on. The one drink turned to several, but none of the three accomplished the goal of tying on a good-time drunk. It simply took the edge off their senses and dulled the memories of the terrible events of the past few days. The celebration the three had anticipated when they left the camp did not materialize. They sat without talking, each soldier absorbed in his own thoughts, quietly sipping the strong drink until one by one they nodded off to sleep.

For Victor it was a restless, dream-laden sleep in which images of fallen soldiers floated through his imagination. He awoke in the cold predawn darkness, with the taste of cheap liquor heavy in his mouth and a chill in his bones. He knew a return to sleep was impossible.

"Wake up! It's time to go. It's almost daylight."

"Go to hell. It's still dark outside," Vincenti said. He had drunk more than the others and had a pretty heavy hangover.

"Hector, help me get Vincenti up. It's time to go."

"Go on, we'll catch up later."

"No. Come on. We're in this together. Anyway, I can't find my way back alone," Victor lied.

They grumbled and complained and finally unfolded their stiff bodies. They got back to camp in time for another hour's sleep before the bugles sounded. The cannons had been pulled up closer to the fort during the night. More soldiers had joined the siege.

Every day the cannons moved closer and more soldiers joined the tightening circle around the Alamo. The Mexican army gave the Texians no peace. The bugles and cannons kept the besieged on edge day and night.

The Texians still suffered no casualties. Every once in a while, a single rider would leave or enter the Texian fortress. One time thirty or so reinforcements came charging into the Alamo, but there was no other significant movement to or from the fortress.

On one occasion during the siege, someone had the idea to cut off the Alamo's water supply by diverting a watering ditch that ran through the grounds. Six men were assigned to the detail. Unfortunately they chose a spot just within range of the Texians' long rifles. Two were shot dead, one wounded, and the others escaped back to their lines. The bombardment continued. The cannons moved closer, the circle tightened around the Alamo, and the Texians still hadn't lost a single man.

"They could have asked anyone from General Cos' troops. We were all here before. Any one of us could have told them that cutting off that little ditch would not have cut off the water supply to the Alamo. Their main water supply is a well inside the grounds."

Vincenti was angry at a condition he diagnosed as officer stupidity. "Damned commissioned officers. If you put all their brains together you still wouldn't have enough to fill a thimble. They should let the non-commissioned officers run the army."

"Two of them that went out were NCO's—a corporal and a sergeant."

"Yeah, but the only reason they were there is because some officer sent them." Hector wasn't about to change Vincenti's opinion about officers.

One day around March 4, Vincenti returned from a NCO meeting. He looked jubilant. "Well boys, it looks like it's about over. I talked with a sergeant who is on the staff of Colonel la Pena who's an *aide-de-camp* to the Generalissimo. We have more troops coming all the time. We'll soon have six thousand against fewer than two hundred. More important, though, in less than a week we'll have several twelve-pound cannons. Twelve-pound cannons can turn that old fort into rubble in about two days' time. Besides that, the Texians are running out of ammunition. You can tell by the way they are rationing it and it is said that there is little food left there. Can you imagine the Texians standing on a pile of rubble, surrounded by thousands of us and without ammunition? What choices do they have? All we have to do is wait a few days and nobody else has to die in a charge."

"Are you sure about this? You know how rumors can develop in the army." Victor was skeptical.

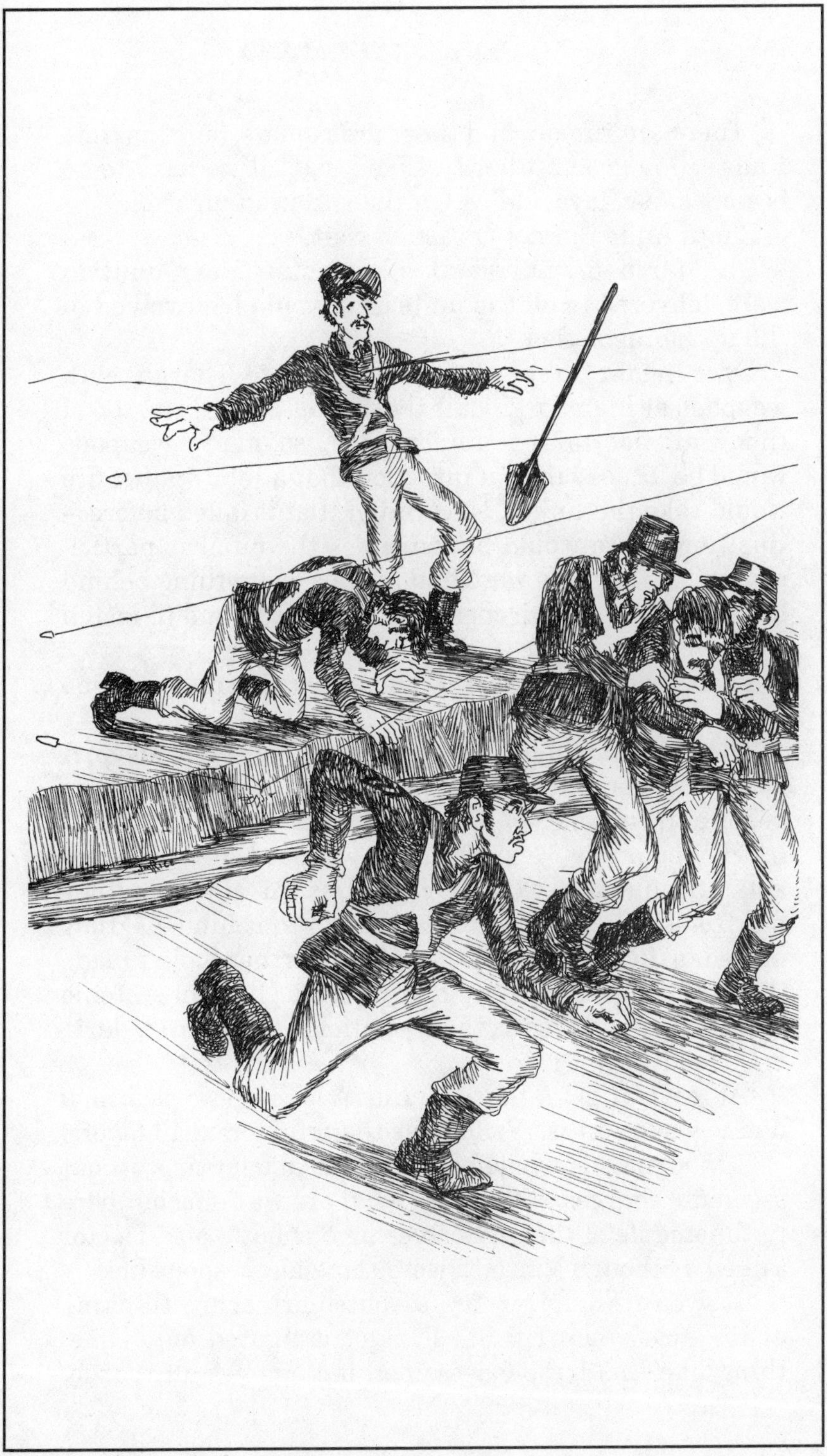

"There are rumors and there are rumors, but this time I have it on good authority. Like I say, all we have to do is wait a few days and watch the situation unravel."

Santa Anna did not choose to wait.

On March 5, individual allotments of ammunition were delivered to all the units that would be involved in the upcoming action.

Once again they were instructed to charge with weapons at high port, point their rifles toward the top of the wall, not taking aim because so many weapons would be focused in that direction that a solid wall of fire would rake the target. Nevermind that it failed before—this time there would be ten times the number participating. The soldiers were told to leave everything behind but their weapons, to check their footwear, and to fasten their chin straps.

That evening there was no cannon barrage and no music, only silence.

The logic was to lull the Texians into a sound sleep. A fresh norther had blown in earlier that evening, so despite the absence of noise, sleep was difficult for those in the open. The Mexican army wrapped in their blankets and huddled close to campfires. At midnight they had to leave those creature comforts behind as they moved up in battle formation. If the norther hadn't made them cold enough, many had to cross the San Antonio River in order to reach their positions. It was cold, dark, and cloudy.

"At least we got a ride on a raft. A lot of those poor men had to wade across." Victor was thankful for small favors.

"I thought this whole business was about over without any more charges. If that's so, what are we doing out here in the middle of the night freezing our butts off?" Hector talked as though Vincenti were somehow responsible.

"I swear, I'll never try to outsmart army thinking again. Just when I think I've got it figured out, something like this happens—something against all reason.

Somebody got in a hurry. Maybe somebody knows more than we thought. Maybe the Texians are out of ammunition. At any rate, it can't take too long with so many of us, and so few of them. Let's go get it over with."

A hoarse whisper interrupted, "Hey—you three—shut up! We're out to surprise the enemy, not alarm him. Silence!"

They assumed prone positions facing the Alamo. It was so cold they had to constantly wiggle their fingers to feel the icy rifles. There was no windbreak to slow the cold wind. It cut right through the tunics that had seemed so hot and heavy at times on the long march. Now they were entirely inadequate against the effects of the blue norther. Rest was impossible. Would their cold, stiff bodies respond when they were called on to react?

Every once in a while they had to move their extremities just to be sure they were still alive. The suspense and coldness made time drag on and on. Most were ready to face anything if it would break the tension. Hours later, around four A.M., they started a slow, creeping movement toward the big, ominous, black shadow looming ahead. As they crawled closer they could see that their objective was that dreaded log barricade guarded by Kwocky and those deadly cannons.

Slowly, slowly they advanced, then the bugles sounded and everyone was in motion in an instant. Guns were all at once firing from both Texian and Mexican lines. Thousands of Mexicans were charging from all sides. The Texian cannons fired and large gaps opened up in the Mexican lines every time one exploded. The three friends stayed close together with Hector, just ahead of the others.

Hector was down. Strange—it appeared he had been hit from behind. Then others, many others, seemed to be shot from behind, taken down by friendly fire. A glance to the rear revealed why. The charging Mexican lines were not raising their rifle barrels enough. Many were

shooting from the waist and hitting their own troops.
Victor tried to stop to help Hector and a cavalry officer
struck him with the flat side of his sword and motioned
him forward.

With bullets striking from both front and rear, Victor
and Vincenti both somehow reached the wall.

There were too few scaling ladders at that point.
Bodies were piling up. To stay there was certain death.
The Texians could not depress their weapons to hit a
target close against the wall, but the friendly fire from
their own side was almost as deadly.

Victor huddled against the wall, frozen in horror. He
couldn't force his body to move in any direction. He
slowly sank to the ground, shaking convulsively.

A hand grasped him by the collar and jerked him
upright, "*Venga,* amigo! You can't stay here. This is a
death trap. We can't go forward." The advancing soldiers
were climbing up the few scaling ladders like ants
swarming up a stick to escape rising water, only to climb
into a blazing fire. The pushing hoard of bodies would
not allow them to retreat. "And we can't go back. That
leaves the side." He pulled Victor along to the west, away
from that part of the defense manned by Kwocky's group
of Tennesseans. Those who found a place on the scaling
ladders were no better off. As soon as they reached the
top, the Texians knocked them down again. A heavy dark
cloud was hanging low over the entire battlefield—a
cloud formed by the burning black gunpowder.
Everybody seemed in a state of wild, confused panic.

Everyone but Vincenti. He alone of the charging
infantry seemed to know what he was doing, or so it
seemed to Victor. The west side wasn't as bad as the
south side, from where they had come, but it was still no
place to loiter so they continued north.

The north showed the most activity. A large hole had
been knocked in the wall on that side and everybody was
being swept into it like swimmers in a current moving

toward a waterfall. It was either move with the crowd or be trampled by it. Near the hole, the surface covering of rock and mortar had been knocked off, revealing cross poles underneath. Those who tried to stay at the base of the wall or those who couldn't find a handhold were crushed against the wall. Victor and Vincenti were separated. It was impossible to distinguish individual faces under the black masks of gunpowder. There were faceless masses of surging bodies pushing forward, yelling, screaming, and shooting.

Victor reached up and grasped one of the crossbars to pull himself out of the melee. He knew that if he went down here it would be the same as being hit with a rifle bullet. There would be no getting up. Bullets thumping into the wall beside him, coming from his own side, reminded him that there was as much danger from Mexicans as from Texians. He pulled with all his strength to free himself from the closely packed bodies of his comrades in arms. It was particularly difficult because some of them were using his body for a handhold. Their clawing hands tried to pull him down that they might go upward. Each thought that confrontation with the Texians could surely be no worse than this hell. He kicked himself free at last and scrambled up just out of reach of those grasping hands. He paused to catch his breath, but the constant thumping of friendly fire against the wall reminded him that hesitation could be deadly. He wasn't sure just how he did it, but somehow he reached the top. His rifle was gone, ripped from its sling on his back by those clawing hands. He picked up another from among the many lying around. At the top, few were taking time to load and fire. Most rifles had become clubs and spears for the bayonets. Victor used his to ward off blows.

At the top was a parapet for a cannon, one the Mexicans had seized and were turning around to fire on the Texians. The bodies of the Texians were strewn around the area. The young commander, Travis, lay with a hole in his forehead. His fancy uniform was now soiled with black gunpowder and blood. Victor was carried along by the charging horde. They no longer looked or acted like human beings. Glazed eyes showed through featureless faces. The army was a massive killing machine, slaughtering and mutilating every Texian in its path, often ripping apart the fallen corpses. The Texians' own cannons were rolled to the doorways of each of the buildings and fired, destroying anyone or anything inside. The cannons at both ends of the compound that had been turned around by the Mexicans to fire back at the Texians were killing more of their own army than Texians.

It was a killing frenzy. The Mexican army was consumed by a blood lust. Officers found it impossible to control the mob. In one room a few civilians, women, children, and two Negro slaves were found huddled in a corner. An officer stopped the mob before it could rip them apart.

Victor slipped into a vacant room out of the line of fire. He saw six shadowy figures in a back corner. One appeared to be a bent old man, and another a boy no older than himself. He strained to see the figures more closely and something struck him from behind, a dizzying blow to the head. He went down and stayed down. In the dim reaches of his consciousness, he seemed vaguely aware of movement around him, but his body would not respond to his commands.

He lay as still as a corpse.

7

So FAR AS HE KNEW he might have been out seconds, minutes, or hours when he was aroused by shouting. *"Alto!*
Enough of this senseless killing!" An old soldier, General
Castrillo, ordered a group of soldiers who were about to
rip apart the six surviving Texians, to stop. Only a senior officer of such rank could have stopped them.

"Young man!" The General motioned to Victor, slowly
raising himself from the floor. "Are you hit?"

"No, I don't think so. Something struck me on the head
but I think I'll be alright."

"Good! Pick up your weapon and come with me to take
these prisoners to the Generalissimo."

Victor had lost his rifle again but there were plenty of
weapons lying around, available for the taking. He
picked up the rifle of a dead soldier.

The older prisoner looked familiar to Victor. His face
was largely obscured under layers of smudge, but those
eyes he had seen somewhere before. Victor suspected the
man was not as old as he appeared. His stooped position
at first gave the impression of age but Victor soon
decided that his posture was the result of an injury or
extreme fatigue.

The General asked, "Do any of you Texians speak
Spanish? *Habla espanol?*"

No one responded so he motioned the prisoners to follow him. "You fall in behind there, Private. I don't think
this bunch has any fight left but you can't always tell by
looking. There'll be someone down at staff to translate.

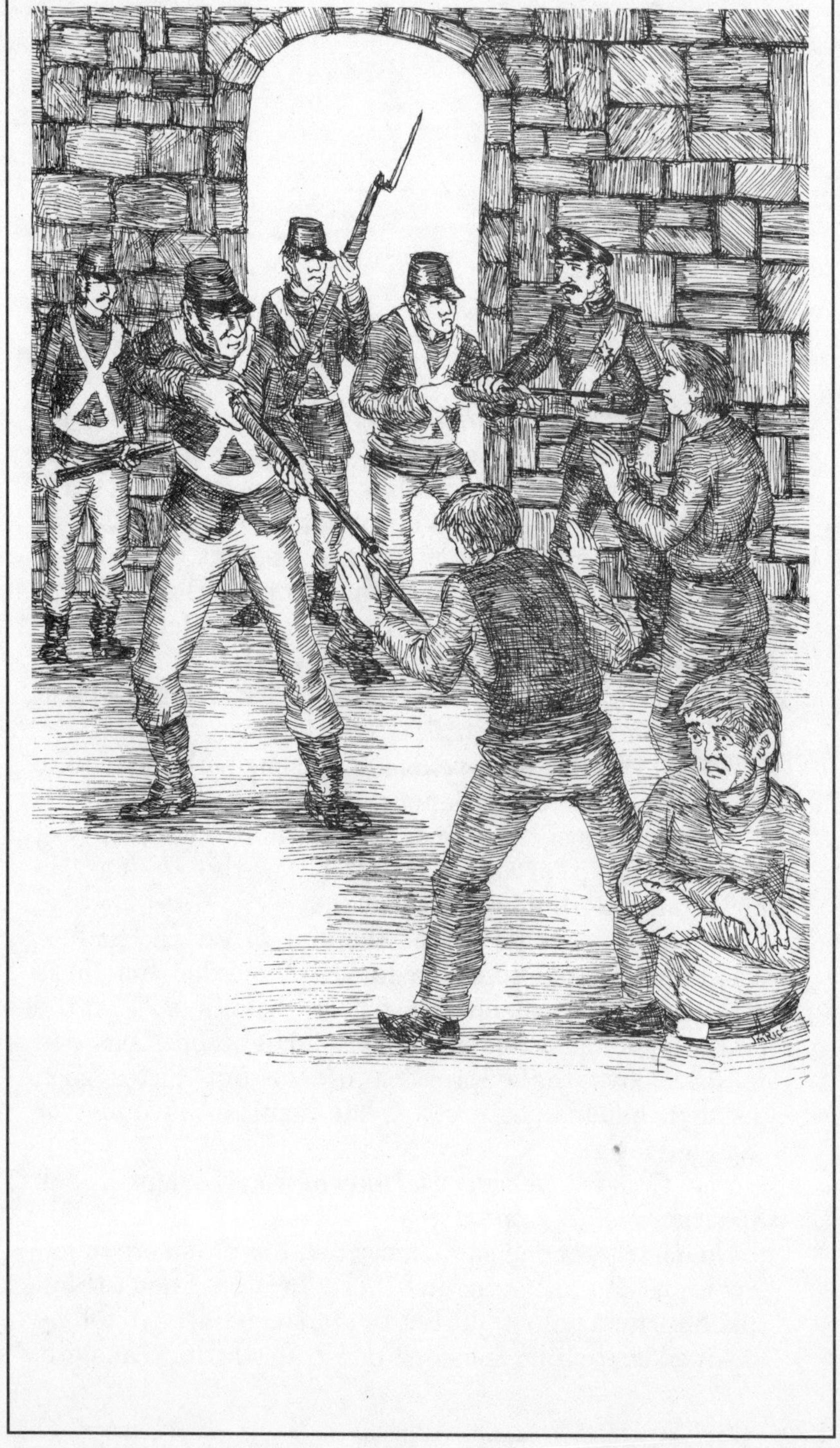

Watch out for our men too, son, they've been caught up in this killing frenzy. Some of 'em just might try to harm the prisoners."

The general led his little detachment of prisoners some distance to the rear. No one cared to challenge a general with an armed escort. Victor was nervous about coming face to face with the famous Santa Anna. Would the Generalissimo recognize him as a former deserter? Would he take a dislike to him on general principles? He need not have worried. The General took no more notice of him than if he had been a piece of furniture.

The oldest prisoner tried frantically to communicate, but neither understood the other's language.

The old man took out a dirty bandana and wiped his face in order to look more presentable. Recognition dawned. It was Kwocky—none other than the infamous Davy Crockett. Victor recognized him from the fandango, and as the figure from the Alamo wall who shot Jose. Victor did not make a public identification—he was too intimidated by the rank of those around him.

Santa Anna was visibly annoyed. "Why did you bring me these prisoners? Did I not say there would be no prisoners?"

General Castrillo spoke, "Sir, Your Excellency, these men put up an honorable fight. They deserve to live. There has been enough killing this day. Killing these miserable creatures would accomplish nothing."

Santa Anna screamed his answer: "We have to teach these rebels a lesson! These are not soldiers. These are outlaws—bandits trying to steal our land. This innocent old man you are protecting is not an innocent old man, this is the famous Davy Crockett! KILL THEM! KILL THEM ALL!"

Without ceremony, the six were taken outside and shot. Their executioners attacked the bodies with bayonets and clubbed them with rifles until there was little left.

Victor was sick.

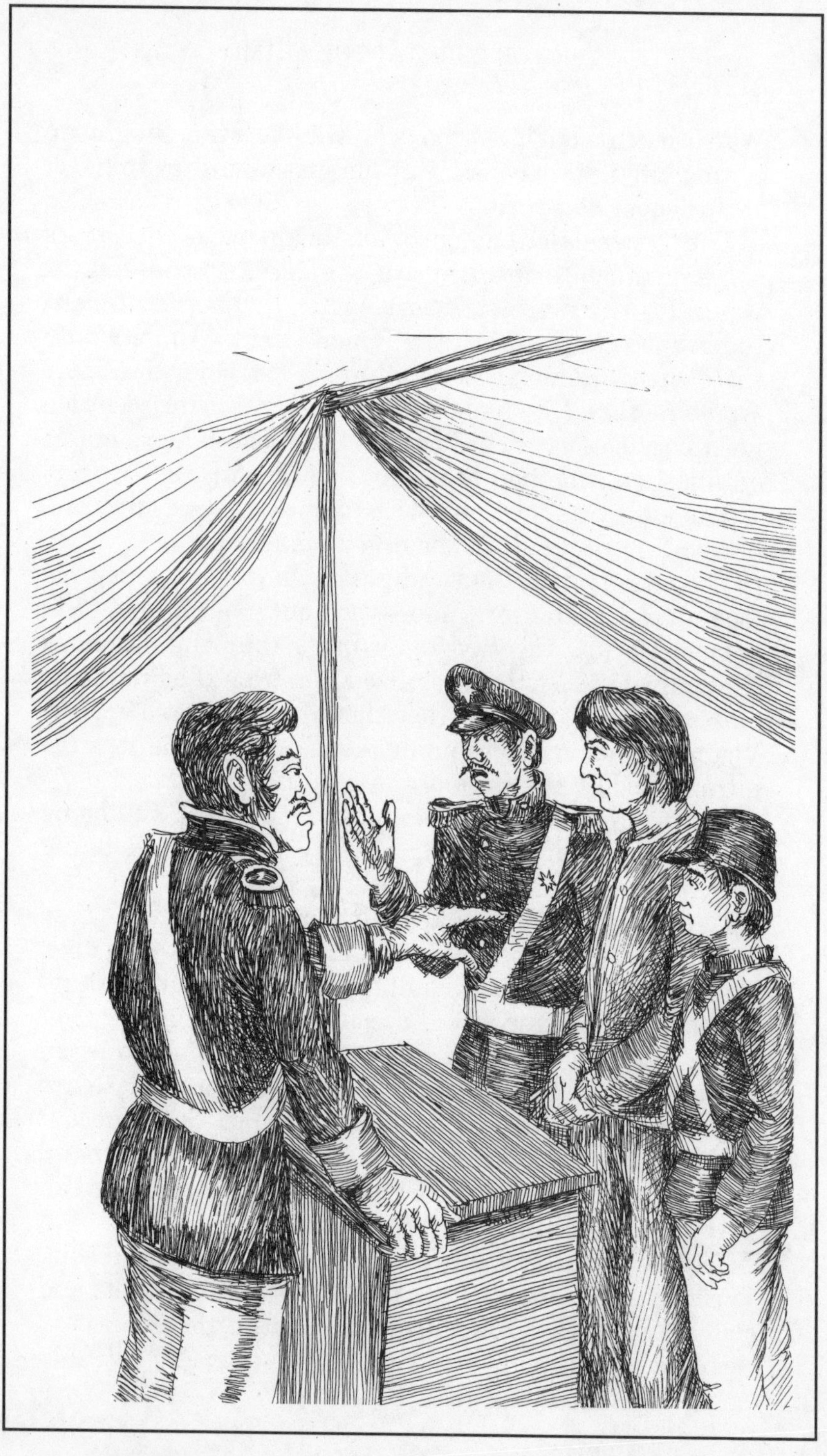

He went back to look for Hector. Where had he seen him go down? Wasn't it just before the south gate?

"No, not there. Here's where he was shot." It was Vincenti speaking from much farther down the battlefield.

"Vincenti! You're alive! I thought everybody I knew was dead." He rushed over to grab Vincenti's hand, a handshake that turned into an embrace.

"Mi hermanito, my little brother! When I saw Hector go down I thought you went down too. It is so good to see you alive. I believe that we are the only two left out of our old squad. It was terrible wasn't it? I believe this was as bad as it gets."

They found Hector's body and Victor wished they hadn't. He had been trampled by the charging troops so he was hardly recognizable by the time they found him.

Details of soldiers were carting bodies to an excavation site for mass burials. Other details were preparing large pyres for burning the Texian dead.

Victor and Vincenti quietly took Hector to his own area, a picturesque location under a large oak tree by the river. Victor made a wooden cross and carved the name and date on the cross bar. Some of the big burial detail had apparently tired of carrying bodies to the burial ground and started dumping them in the river. They backed up and clogged the flow at the bend. Many of the bodies, frozen in grotesque positions, floated by as Victor and Vincenti finished putting away their fallen comrade's remains.

The burial and cremation details continued for days afterward. The Texian bodies were placed between layers of brush and firewood. The smell of burning human flesh was overwhelming. Santa Anna gave the women survivors and the Negro slaves of Travis and Bowie each two silver pesos and a blanket. He promised each of the wounded survivors a bonus, then left with the main force in pursuit of Houston, wherever he might be. He did not leave the promised bonus. He left others to deal with the dead and wounded.

General Cos' regiment was the one left behind to take care of cleanup details and to explain to the wounded why their bonuses were not forthcoming.

The cleanup was completed in about a week. Out of more than fifteen hundred soldiers directly involved in the Mexican attack, over five hundred were killed outright, and many more were wounded. The entire Texian force of one hundred eighty-two was killed.

Santa Anna was invincible. Nobody could stand up to him.

Sam Houston would soon learn his lesson.

The Mexican army had been hearing about a big man named Sam Houston whom the Texians seemed to regard as some sort of superman, but he never seemed to be where the fighting was. He always moved just beyond the action. Some said he was trying to raise an army among those ragtag Texians. They had no organization, no uniforms, and not enough weapons to go around. Santa Anna had one of the best armies in the world. Sam Houston could run just so long. Sooner or later they would corner the elusive rebel and his unruly mob and devour them like wolf on a lamb.

The insolent fool from the north would soon learn his lesson. With Houston out of the way, the rest of the Texians would soon fall into line. Sam Houston could be a force to reckon with, but there was no way he could raise an army with the power to face an opponent such as Santa Anna. He simply didn't have the resources to face a real army.

8

Santa Anna divided his army into thirds to hunt down the Texian army under Sam Houston. He took the largest group of sixteen hundred troops and went toward the Gulf of Mexico where the San Jacinto River emptied by way of Harrisburg and New Washington. He hoped to corner Houston with his back to the Gulf and hemmed in by river, stream, and swamp.

General Cos, with his brigade of four hundred troops, followed the route of Santa Anna, who they would join near the Gulf.

The long march began. In many respects it was the same as before and yet it was so much different. It was the same long hours, the same cumbersome load, the same uncomfortable uniforms, and the same miserable army rations. But this time the marchers were tough hardened soldiers. The weather was beautiful, and they traveled through more populated areas with more opportunity for foraging to supplement the army rations.

"It's a terrible thing to have lost such a battle after marching so far," Victor spoke to Vincenti.

"Lost? What do you mean lost? This was a great victory for Mexico!"

"How could we have won! We had three times the number of casualties the Texians had." Victor was astonished at the logic that would attribute a victory to a group who had so many more casualties.

"The way the officers count a victory is not who loses fewer men, but who has the most standing at the end of

the conflict. Lives lost are not important so long as it is
not their own. That is one of the reasons I hold all officers in such low regard. I think I may have killed three
Texians myself. How many did you get?"

"I didn't get any, I'm afraid. I didn't get my rifle to
work. It jammed I guess." He didn't say he didn't know
how to load and shoot the weapon, no one had shown
him how. "About the only use I got from the rifle was
keeping the Texians from hitting me, until I got hit from
behind."

"Judging from what you said before, you entered that
room after most of the fighting was over. I wouldn't be
surprised if you were hit by one of our own troops. Some
of them were acting pretty crazy about that time. They
were hitting out at anything that moved. We are both
lucky to be here alive."

The weather had changed. Spring had finally arrived
in southern Texas. It was hard to remain in a depressed
state of mind amid the beauty of the new season.
Wildflowers painted the landscape and filled the atmosphere with their perfume. The whole world was fresh
and new. It was impossible not to be affected.

"What are we going to do when we get to Gonzales?"
Vincenti was thinking about the good times they could
have in the nearest sizeable town since San Antonio.

"I guess we'll just have to wait and see what it has to
offer. Anything has to be better than San Antonio after
the battle. We need something to get rid of the smell of
death." As far as Victor was concerned, everything connected with San Antonio was one horrible nightmare.

Most of the farmhouses they passed were deserted, so
foraging was good. There were pantries to be robbed and
chicken houses to be raided. Most of the cattle had been
chased off, away from the route of the marchers, but the
pickings were still good.

Near Gonzales they found farmhouses burned and
food supplies destroyed. Gonzales was razed to the

ground. Everything of value to the invading army was used, destroyed, or ruined beyond further use.

"I guess we've found out what Gonzales has to offer . . . nothing. Why would anybody do this? Why would anybody destroy everything they have?" Victor was befuddled.

"I believe it would be a safe guess that these Texians don't like us very well. I suppose this is better than having them shoot at us. They are out to deny us the spoils of war. They would do without themselves rather than share with the enemy."

Outside Gonzales, more houses were left standing and not so much property was destroyed. General Cos' troops were encouraged to roam out from the main line of march, to augment their army issue supplies, particularly rations.

On such a foraging expedition, Victor and Vincenti came upon a deserted house. The occupants had left very hurriedly, so much so that they left a meal served but uneaten on the dining room table. The food wasn't hot but it was plentiful. The two ate most of what was prepared for a large family.

"This is the good part of being in the army. As a civilian, where in the world would you find such luxury as this? The fact that we had to endure such hardships makes it all the more meaningful. I don't know too much about the glory and country and principles I hear about. It makes you feel deeper, to appreciate the good times, having known the opposite extreme. There is excitement and terror. It's living on the edge between life and death. It sharpens the senses."

Vincenti went on about life in the military but Victor's concerns were about the immediate situation, "I don't know about all that. This fried chicken, potatoes, and biscuits are as good as can be. I would just as soon do without the excitement on the other end. If we ever get out of this mess, I'll stick with my plan to be a vaquero. I'd rather chase cows than Texians. I wish you'd come in with me. Jose had it figured out when we get out of the army we'll have some of this Texian land coming for ourselves. If we put our land together we'd have enough to start a good little ranch."

"You and your cattle ranch. That sounds like too much work for me. Come on, let's see what else of value we can find around here."

The people who had left the house were rich, by Victor and Vincenti's standards. They found a bathtub, cleaned up, and finished the job with generous splashes of good-smelling cologne.

They awoke several hours later and made their way back to the kitchen. They enjoyed another meal and after-dinner cigars from a box Vincenti had found while foraging. Victor didn't enjoy the cigar as much as he pretended, but he wanted to appear mature in front of Vincenti.

"This sure is a good cigar. This has been a really nice side trip to distract from the war. I could get used to this. What's to keep us from just staying here and letting the soldiers and war go on without us?"

"There's two big reasons, the Texians and the Mexicans. Texians will be looking out to avenge the Alamo. They would shoot us on sight. It is not good business to shoot the prisoners we did because the situation can be reversed so easily. The Mexican army would shoot us for deserters if they found us. Either way is not good besides, how are you going to get land for your cattle ranch if you do not stay in the army and get your veterans' land grant that's sure to be forthcoming? Who knows, you might get as a grant this very house and land we are occupying now."

"I was just speculating, I know the consequences of going against the Generalissimo."

"Well, if we're going to rejoin the army we had better prepare to leave the good life and catch up."

They stuffed their pockets with cigars, dried fruits, and candy. Vincenti strapped on a sword he found and he

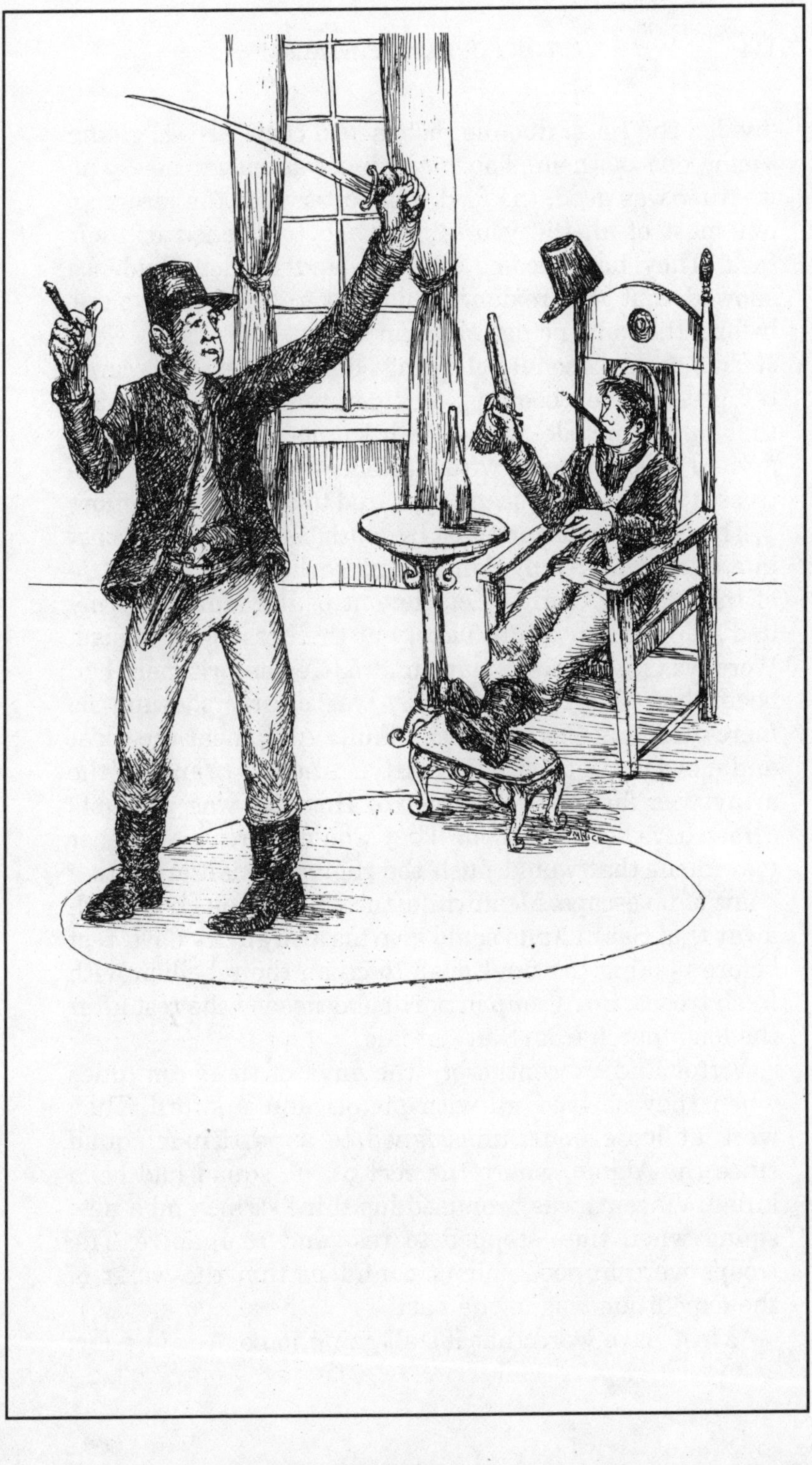

divided the set of dueling pistols he'd come across, giving Victor one of them. The marching was easier now. The weather was good, the food was better with the foraging, but most of all the young men had toughened to their task. They had become stronger and harder. Evidence showed that the Texian civilians were fleeing in panic before the advancing Mexican army. The roads were strewn with personal belongings discarded by the scared refuges—clothes, bedding, cooking utensils, and anything that might impede their forward progress. In places the ground was so strewn with white feathers from torn mattresses that the landscape appeared to be covered in snow.

The march continued east by southeast toward the coast in a route followed by Santa Anna earlier after the Battle of the Alamo. Another detachment of the Mexican army had scored a significant victory at the Presidio at Goliad. Word was that around four hundred Texian prisoners had been shot. The Mexican army was clearly showing no mercy. General Cos would join Santa Anna near the coast and move north to corner Houston. Another branch of the army was farther to the north. Houston was probably somewhere between them. They would exercise a pincher movement that would push the ragtag Texian army to a point of no escape. Meanwhile, the enemy was far enough away that Santa Anna could give his army a few days' rest before making the final push to crush the rebellion with fresh troops. Cos' group in particular needed the rest after the long march from San Antonio.

Victor and Vincenti were the envy of their comrades when they showed up with pistols and a sword. They were at loose ends, unassigned to a particular squad since the Alamo, where the rest of the squad had been killed. Vincenti was promised his third stripe and a new squad when they stopped to rest and reorganize. The troops were in good spirits, confident that the worst of the expedition was in the past.

"I just have word that it's all going to be over in a few

days. We're getting close. We'll get paid and have a few days' liberty near one of these coastal towns. I hear they can get pretty wild, a lot wilder than San Antonio, I hear."

"This has been an easy march compared with before San Antonio, but it will be nice to stay in one place for a few days without worrying about somebody shooting at you."

"I've got something to show you." Vincenti took a folded piece of cloth from his knapsack and spread it over a large flat rock. It was an elaborately embroidered tablecloth he'd taken from the deserted farmhouse. He took out the candlestick holder, a candle, and a box of fancy biscuits. "We dine in style tonight. We'll join Santa Anna tomorrow. In a few days we'll be eating fancy foods and drinking fine wine for real in the company of beautiful women. Well, at least at this stage of the game, most women we meet we would consider beautiful . . . we won't have to pretend much longer."

They nibbled on the gourmet biscuits and sipped water from canteen cups like it was wine.

That night they slept and dreamed of the good days ahead.

They were up early and on the march. The terrain was swampy with streams connected to the bay. Santa Anna's troops were camped on an open, grassy plain in the crook of one of the streams. His camp could be reached only by crossing over several hundred yards of the grassy plain. No enemy could approach without being seen at this great distance, allowing plenty of time for the alarm to be sounded and the troops alerted. Houston and his army were far to the north anyway . It was a semi-permanent camp with tents erected and cooking facilities set up for hot meals.

General Cos had his troops set up camp and line up for a hot midday meal, an unaccustomed luxury for soldiers in the field.

It was April 21, just two months since they had arrived in San Antonio, and about three months since

Victor had been conscripted into the army. It seemed that other life was remote, far away, something that had happened to someone else. Could he ever go back to that other, simpler life, after the experience of the past three months? No, he didn't think so.

After the hot, leisurely meal, they were treated to another unaccustomed luxury: the afternoon siesta. No one performed anything resembling military duties. Victor and Vincenti slept for awhile and awoke a short time before three o'clock. They sat relaxing in the shade of a large oak tree. The cool shade felt good on this warm Spring day. Vincenti produced the last of his cigars and they lit up. He spoke, "Do you see what I mean about the spoils of war? You can't get much better than this, can you? It wouldn't be nearly so good if we hadn't had some rough times for comparison."

"I have to admit this is pretty good, but I still think I would like to be a vaquero one day. Do we have more reinforcements coming today? They seem in an awful big hurry to get here." Victor indicated a long line of men trotting toward them across the open grassy prairie.

"The idiots. Don't they know that in the army when you have an opportunity to take a break and rest, you take advantage of it? Oh, good lord! Those aren't reinforcements—those aren't our soldiers! Those are Tex . . . "

Vincenti did not finish his sentence.

Victor knew the sound of hard bullets hitting soft flesh. Vincenti's reaction to the shot told him he could be of no aid. It didn't even enter his mind to go for his weapon and take defensive action. Pure terror and raw panic took over his whole being. The Texians were charging with incredible speed. There was no time to think or consider any other form of action.

Victor ran.

9

THE TEXIANS were everywhere, shooting, stabbing, and clubbing. Two small cannons threw pieces of cut-up horseshoes through the retreating troops, chopping them to pieces. It was another killing frenzy like that at the Alamo, but with the sides reversed. Few Mexicans even attempted to retaliate. Most reacted like Victor. They were not allowed to surrender. The Texians would shout back something about Alamo and Goliad and cut them down. Many tried to swim the river or creek to safety as the Texians destroyed the bridge. Sharpshooters stood on the bank and picked swimmers off before they could reach the opposite bank. Victor ran first in one direction, then in the other. There was no safe place to hide or even to pause for a moment to catch his breath. He couldn't think. His mind refused to function. All he could do was react.

He ran through a thicket. The thorns ripped through his clothing and exposed flesh to be scratched and torn. The thicket stopped and he was suddenly slipping, sliding, and then rolling down a muddy creek bank. Floating in the creek there were corpses of those who had tried to swim or wade across. The Texian sharpshooters on the bank did not miss. He moved as quickly as he could under the bank. Just ahead was a clump of bushes growing near the top of the bank. Maybe it would provide a hiding place. Bullets were flying everywhere, most from Texian guns, but as far as he could tell no one had picked him out as a target.

He clawed his way up the bank to the bushes and lost some more skin getting to the midst of the clump where it would seem to offer some degree of cover. He was sure of one thing: he wouldn't be able to continue running much longer. He was lucky in his choice of a hiding place. High water in the past had hollowed out some space behind the bushes. The space was too small for comfort, but the earth was soft enough that he could dig the hole larger with his bare hands. In a few minutes he could squeeze back into the cavity and by bracing his feet against the base of the largest bush, he could hold him-self in place with relative ease.

For the first time since the attack, he could slow down enough to reflect on what was happening. He didn't like his conclusions. The Mexican soldiers were in a complete state of confusion. They were offering only token resist-ance to the Texians who were on the same kind of killing rampage the Mexicans had been on back at the Alamo. They were out for revenge and their blood lust would not likely be satisfied until all opposition was crushed. They were showing no mercy, just as Santa Anna had shown no mercy earlier.

A horseman approached on the bank above him. He could only hope his cover was sufficient to keep him hid-den from his view. He pushed himself as far back against the bank as he could, trying as nearly as possible to become a part of the bank.

The voices came to him clearly but he couldn't under-stand the strange language. The conversational tones of their voices suggested they weren't aware of his pres-ence just below them. If he could only hold out a few hours, maybe he could escape under cover of darkness. It seemed hours since the attack had started but actually it had been less than half an hour. Could he hold out and remain undetected for another three to four hours? His life depended on his doing just that. His leg was cramped and his arm went to sleep but he held on. He needed to move his limbs to keep the circulation going, but he dared not make any sort of movement. A fly crawled across his nose and the cramped leg twitched uncontrollably. The fly crawled up his nose. He needed to sneeze but he couldn't. Another problem arose. The base of the bush where his foot pressed was loosening. The soft earth was releasing its hold on the roots of the plant. This was cause for real concern. If the root loosened, he'd fall down the bank where there would be no escape.

He heard horses move away from the bank above. He started to relax, and then he heard the snort of another horse from the same area. Apparently not all the horses had left.

Why had one of the horsemen stayed behind? Did they suspect he was nearby? They must not know his exact location; otherwise they would simply have shot into the clump of bushes until they hit their target. He wished he knew their language.

All he could do was wait and wonder, wonder if the next second he would be discovered and shot to pieces to avenge the Alamo and Goliad. How could he make them understand that he hadn't killed anyone? In his flight he had seen dozens of his comrades throwing up their hands and shouting *"Me no Alamo, Me no Goliad,"* only to be cut down by Texian bullets, knives, and rifle butts. Just as Santa Anna had shown no mercy, he knew he could expect no mercy.

Victor was cramped and uncomfortable but apparently safe for the moment, as long as the bush remained rooted to the bank. If that horseman above him would go away, he could relax. His body ached to change positions but he dared not move. More important than moving to ease the cramped muscles, he needed to move to take weight off the loosening root. He tried to push still farther into the slight excavation but he could not shift his body to take significant weight off the slowly uprooting bush. He dug his hands into the earth, but he realized the it would not support his weight.

Suddenly the whole shelf of the bank on which the bushes grew gave way and fell in a big chunk. Bush, earth, and Victor fell in a heap, tumbling into the creek bed.

The Texian saw him; of course, his horse was almost caught in the small landslide.

Victor knew he was discovered when he looked up to see the sky filled with the figure of the big Texian on horseback, charging down the bank toward him.

He didn't try a last minute plea for mercy. He did not shout *"Me no Alamo."* He had seen the futility of those gestures by his comrades. The muddy water of the creek bank blurred his vision but he could make out the image of the Texian's raised hand. He could not distinguish what kind of weapon the hand held, whether he was to be shot, clubbed, or stabbed; he couldn't foretell. He squeezed his eyes shut and braced his body for the oncoming blow.

—◦•◦—

Victor felt himself swinging through the air, hanging by the scruff of his neck. He landed on his stomach with such force that it knocked his breath away. He felt himself moving in a bouncing, jarring, sliding motion and realized he had been tossed unceremoniously upon the horse's back, behind the saddle like a bag of oats or a blanket roll. The Texian's firm handhold on his tunic collar was all that kept him from falling. He couldn't worry about his immediate fate. His only concern for the moment was the return of his breath.

He mercifully passed out. He didn't know how long he'd been out when he started coming around again. The Texian saw his passenger was moving so he stopped and let him get into a more comfortable sitting position behind the saddle. At last Victor got a clear look at his captor. He was a big man, wide of shoulder and narrow of hip, probably in his late twenties. His clear, gray eyes focused sharply under overhanging brows. His features

were etched in hard lines accented by a sandy handlebar mustache to give his face a fierce demeanor. Closer observation suggested weariness, a deep-down fatigue underneath the tough exterior.

Neither had spoken a word. Victor didn't know the language of his captor and there was no reason to believe the Texian knew his.

They didn't seem to be following any kind of road or trail as far as Victor could tell, but the big Texian seemed to know exactly where he was going. The sun set, the moon rose and they rode on into the night. Victor was dozing in the saddle and near falling off the horse when they finally stopped somewhere in a little clearing surrounded by trees and brush. In the moonlight Victor could make out a small cabin and outbuildings with log fences designed to hold livestock.

The Texian took care of the horse and they went inside. He moved about, lighting a lamp, stirring up a fire, and starting the coffee with a practiced familiarity. He knew the cabin well.

The Texian spoke his first words since their meeting. Victor was surprised to hear him speak in perfect Spanish, "This is my house, do you like it? My name is John Daugherty."

"I am called Victor Lopez. Yes, it's a nice house. Why did you save me?"

John poured coffee for the two. "You don't look like a very dangerous person to me. I'd heard about the terrible atrocities at the Alamo and Goliad. I, like most Texans, was furious. I wanted revenge. Then came this last battle, the battle of San Jacinto. I saw our people acting the same as I heard about Santa Anna's soldiers. I don't think either army's behavior was anything to brag about. Honor? Nobility? Bull. I am sick of this whole business that turns men into unthinking killing machines, worse than wild beasts. I left a family up north and came down here to make a good life in a new country. I came to farm a few acres and run some cattle, not get in the middle of a shooting war for God's sake. How'd you get mixed up in all this mess?"

Victor told him the story about being abducted, pushed into battle without even being shown how to use his weapon and even about his plans of going into the cattle business with his new friends.

"Ha! They didn't even show you how to shoot your gun, huh? They can't blame you for killing our people. I'm afraid I can't make the same boast about not killing anybody, but I'm not proud of it. That Santa Anna's a real monster, isn't he? I hope they hang him high."

"So you want to be a vaquero, eh? What do you know about running cattle?"

"We used to have our little farm where we had a milk cow and some goats . . . "

John laughed. He threw back his head and laughed a deep-down, belly-shaking laugh. "Well, I guess everybody has to start somewhere. It happens that I do need some help and I can't afford to pay anyone. I have my own boy coming down, but he's just six and he wouldn't be much help. If you want to work for beans and beef, a place to sleep, and a share of the profits sometime in the future, if there are any profits, then I've got a job for you."

The big Texan was offering Victor a chance to pursue a dream.

Santa Anna surely wouldn't be in the position to make land grants to his veterans now. In light of Santa Anna's behavior in other situations, the idea that he would offer such rewards to his soldiers was most likely a pipe dream from the beginning.

Victor could always return home to his mother and uncle in their little *caseta,* to a peaceful life dominated by love. He longed to see his mother, the old man, and his animals.

But he couldn't.

He had seen the elephant the old soldiers spoke of so

often. Once one saw the elephant, they said, one could never go back. He would never again be satisfied with what was before. There was a whole world out there and Victor had seen only a small corner of it.

The big Texan asked again. "Well, do you want to go with me and work the cattle?"

Victor answered, "*Si,* señor."